RISKY BUSINESS

JB TREPAGNIER

Edited by Iwordynerdy

Cover by Hannah Stern-Jakob Designs

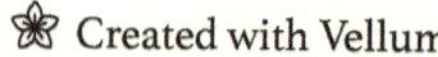 Created with Vellum

RISKY BUSINESS

And then Daddy Dearest enters stage left.

So, I met my father. I beat the crap out of him, but I haven't killed him yet. Yet being the operative word. I still haven't made up my mind about that. I had my to-do list before I broke out of Scorchwood and killing him was a major part of my big kill list. I mean, the man framed me, sent me to prison in Hell, then had a mad warlock experiment on me.

When you're fate's little bitch, you kind of have to expect the unexpected. And my father's big reveal about why he did all those horrible things to me and everyone else was like that movie where that kid sees dead people. I didn't see it coming.

So, now we are uneasy allies. The fate of two realms is resting on my shoulders. That doesn't mean I might not still decide to kill him if we manage to pull this off.

SERAFINA

I did not understand what was happening to me. I hesitated to kill my father because I needed to know so badly why he had done all of this. I needed him to look me in the eyes and tell me why he didn't stop when he realized who I was to him. Call me stupid. I wasn't expecting some tearful reunion. We were well past that. I just wanted to know why.

I wasn't expecting his answer. It didn't make me feel any better, and I wasn't any less pissed off at what he did to me. If anything, I was angrier at him. He let me beat him, and he kept looking at me like he was so fucking *proud* of me. Proud of what exactly? He didn't know me from his asshole. All he knew about me was what Rathmore reported to him and that I broke out of that stupid prison and took all his test subjects away.

I should have killed him, but Fae couldn't lie, and if he was telling the truth, then the one place that actually felt like home to me was in danger. I had no choice but to ask him to portal us back to Zepar's estate and fill everyone else in.

Stopping everyone from killing him was a huge cluster-fuck, especially since he decided to announce himself by kidnapping me to the Fae realm. I didn't get a tour, and I didn't want one. As soon as one of those Fae bastards realized I was a halfling, they would just execute me.

Eiltan explained Zepar had somehow made all the Fae women barren and would only give him the cure if the Fae helped him become king of Hell. I still wasn't sure how a hybrid baby was supposed to help with that.

Amduscias was pacing and kept running his fingers through his black hair. I knew he wanted to get back to Hell and tell Bael what was going on, but we still didn't have the full story from my father. I had so many questions I didn't know where to start.

"Why didn't you bring this straight to Hell?" Amduscias demanded. "Every fire born demon has unique powers. Zepar is not that strong for a fire born. His legion is small and weak. His demonic abilities are to make people fall in love, but he can also make women barren. Why were you trying to mix demon blood with an elemental?"

"I only let a few trusted people in on this," Eiltan said. "You don't understand. This was a significant error on my part. It took me a long time to grow up and act like a prince. Finding a remedy for the sick Fae was the first real responsibility my father trusted me with. It was my idea to ask Hell for help. It was voted upon, and everyone agreed with my idea. They warned me not to do anything to offend any of the kings of Hell when I asked.

"I was so nervous about it. I hadn't been born yet the last time my family negotiated with the kings of Hell. I was told the demons were all gracious and kind but fierce when it came to contracts. We Fae pride ourselves in always winning when we make a deal, but I knew they made concessions during that contract. I know my family doesn't enjoy discussing that contract because it didn't go totally to our liking.

"I came into the human realm first to decide how I would approach this. Unlike my family, I think we should reopen the portal, and the descendants of our blood recognized and welcomed into the Fae world should they want to. I've always found this sort of peace and chaos when I cross the portal.

"Zepar must have been watching and monitoring for any Fae to cross because it was he who approached me first. I was eating dinner, and he sat down at my table as if I had invited him. He introduced himself as a Duke of Hell.

"I knew my father would expect the deal to be made with the kings and not a Duke. Always go straight to who is in charge, or a deal can be broken. I tried to get a feel for the kings by chatting to Zepar about how to handle myself. He seemed very friendly and willing to help.

"That was when he dropped a bomb on me. He told me the kings of Hell were upset that they were not included in the contracts when my ancestors turned Scorchwood into a general prison. He thought they would be unwilling to help us after that. But he told me he could get me a remedy, and Hell would never have to know. All he would ask in return was that he would ask a favor from me later.

"I knew better. I really did. That kind of deal is below the Fae. We only make those kinds of deals when *we* are the ones asking for favors later. I didn't want to fail since going to Hell was my big idea. I wanted to save my people. My family wasn't proud of that contract, but they had a lot of respect for the kings of Hell for their negotiation skills and always said they had honor.

"I thought since Zepar was a Duke, he would too. I agreed with his terms. He delivered and brought us vials of a potion that cured the sickness. I saved two vials of it and gave it to Fae scientists to see if they could synthesize it in case the illness came back. We came close, but there was one ingredient we couldn't make. The potion had demon blood in it.

"At the time, I thought it was necessary to cure our people. It seemed to work, and everyone was healthy. But as time passed and Fae started having difficulty conceiving, a close confidant who knew what I did thought it might have had something to do with the demon blood in the potion.

"I started making several trips topside under the guise of gathering human research to help our women, but I was looking for Zepar. I managed to find his estate. I met Serafina's mother while I was trying to gain an audience with him.

"Serafina, despite what you may think, she wasn't a fling. We took every precaution so she wouldn't fall pregnant because I didn't want my child in danger from my father. I even loved her.

"I still had to make frequent trips back home with human science. I was close to meeting with Zepar again when I had to leave to report my findings. I *had* to leave. I intended to come right back, but my father ordered me to stay because he thought someone was plotting against him.

"By the time I got back, Ava was gone. I thought she was furious at me for being gone for so long and went somewhere I couldn't find her. I had no reason to suspect she was pregnant. We were cautious. Believe me, Serafina. If I had known, I would have done what I needed so you both survived the birth, and I would have made sure you had a very different upbringing."

"Bullshit," I snapped. I knew he couldn't lie, but maybe he just thought he meant that. "As soon as you found out who I was, you let your mad warlock experiment on me. You had no problem with me being one of your test subjects. You didn't even ask me if I wanted a child."

"Why do you think a child with diluted Fae blood and demon blood will cure your people?" Amduscias asked.

"We thought we could synthesize it into a cure. We would never have hurt the baby. We would have taken blood, and that was it."

"None of this is making sense," Skoll said. "My blood and Roman's blood were in Rathmore's lab. Why all the other hybrids if you just needed one?"

Eiltan cleared his throat. He'd better have a suitable explanation for that because there were so many holes in his story, I could make a swiss cheese sandwich out of it.

"Jasmine was arrested legitimately, and so was her gang. It was only ever supposed to be with people who ended up there naturally. Jasmine was supposed to be focusing on seducing Amduscias, but he turned her down. She consoled herself by taking a wolf to her bed. Jasmine needed to know she was desirable, so every time Amduscias ignored her, she took another lover.

"By all rights, she should have fallen pregnant with a hybrid baby, even if the child didn't have demon blood. When I am king, I plan on opening the portal to Earth again. My trusted advisor was curious about why Jasmine hadn't fallen pregnant at all. By all reports, she had many lovers, and she had sex every day, sometimes multiple times.

"When I open the portal again, I don't want to deny my people love. When we were here before, the Fae only took human lovers. But what would happen if they fell in love with a Vampire or shifter? Would they be able to have children?"

"How does framing people play into that?" Roman growled. "Your pet warlock tortured me and put a spell on my brain, so I was his killing machine."

"Please, Rathmore was never my idea. I thought he was an evil man. Warden Skinner insisted with the right training, he could help and that she could control him. I had no idea he tortured you or that he put a control spell on Serafina, or I would have ordered his execution myself. Warden Skinner was the one who reported all the progress from the prison."

"Ask him why elementals and not pure Fae women, Ena."

"Why didn't you just have a willing Fae woman instead of framing elementals?"

Eiltan's shoulders slumped, and he sighed.

"What you must think of me, my child. I didn't set out to frame anyone. It was always supposed to be women who ended up there naturally. Warden Skinner was supposed to pull everyone aside and get their consent to take part in exchange for freedom.

"Because of their Fae blood, the justice system looks the other way quite often when one commits crimes. I did not understand why we had so many elemental inmates recently until Serafina was arrested, and I found out Warden Skinner was handpicking them and framing them. I only found that out when you escaped and killed Rathmore. I knew something was going on under my nose.

"I only just found out they framed everyone. I'm setting things in motion to have her fired, and I was on my way to visit all the elementals in safe houses to let them know they could leave. I was clearing their names. One man reported his charge just disappeared into the shadows, so I knew demons kidnapped them.

"I checked both of Zepar's estates in case it was him that took them. I found all of you here, so I decided to whisk my daughter away so I could finally meet her and explain myself. This was never supposed to go this far. It was only ever supposed to happen with willing inmates who had given their consent. I couldn't bring a Fae woman in because they simply can't conceive anymore, and none of the elementals I approached topside wanted to mix with a demon."

Amduscias flipped his hair out of his eyes.

"You didn't have *my* consent. No one ever approached me about making a hybrid baby with an inmate. I would never have gone along with it."

Eiltan sighed.

"I'm sorry. I was told you had given your consent as long as the elemental was someone you cared about."

"Your plan never would have worked, anyway. The only thing that can reverse what was done to your women is Zepar. It's his blood that made them barren, and it's his blood that has to reverse it. You can't just pick a demon and use their blood to reverse what a fire born has done."

"Zepar isn't going to help us unless I send a Fae army to attack Hell," Eiltan said.

"Which is why we are going to Hell right now. You are going to explain to the kings exactly what is going on and why. You will tell them anything you might have learned about Zepar. His legion is all inferior spirits, and he doesn't have that many. He can't overthrow the monarchy with what he has. If Zepar is blackmailing you for an army, there's no telling who else he's managed to get on his side."

Why was my father so cooperative? I still hadn't

processed what he said about loving my mother and not knowing about me. It was a little too late to think about what my life might have been like if he had returned a little faster, and she was able to discuss her pregnancy with him.

"I don't expect any of you to forgive me, but I want to help you stop Zepar. I'll go to Hell and help in any way I can. I'll accept any punishment the kings deem worthy."

"Get the other elementals," Amduscias said. "Now that we know this entire mess is because Zepar fucked over the Fae to get an army, I don't want them here at his estate. We have to get everyone to Hell."

Great. We'd just spent all this time trying to convince them to stay at Zepar's place because my father was evil. My father was still a dick, but now we were asking them to go to Hell with us because Zepar had been the bad guy all along.

FERGUS

Something wasn't right. I knew Eiltan couldn't lie, so how did he not know what was going on at the prison if I heard that conversation with Warden Skinner where he knew she was gassed and kidnapped? What was all that about consent when, by definition, gassing someone to capture them and run tests on them was non-consent?

Skoll had gone to get our missing elementals while Serafina and Amduscias continued to ply Eiltan with questions.

"Ena, if he says he didn't know, I overheard him speaking to Warden Skinner. He knew they gassed the prison and kidnapped you. He was betting on you not remembering."

"I thought he couldn't lie."

"He can't. He's telling the truth, but something isn't adding up. Ask him."

My Ena squared her shoulders and glared at him.

"If everything at Scorchwood was Warden Skinner's

doing, then something isn't right. You knew I was kidnapped and tested. You didn't want me to remember."

Eiltan frowned. He didn't know about me, but he also wanted to know how she knew that.

"You were supposed to be taken in your sleep and given Fae vaccines. There are still diseases that can kill us, and I wanted to make sure you had the vaccines you would have had if I knew about you. Did that not happen?"

I growled. No, that didn't happen. And why did they need to gas the entire prison for vaccines? Why was she warded if they thought she knew nothing about what was going on and would have accepted being walked out the jail for a few shots?

"I was drugged and given a pelvic exam."

Now Eiltan was growling. He really was furious about this. None of this was making sense.

"Rathmore was *not* supposed to do that. He was supposed to take a blood sample so I could see what immunities you had and give you some needed vaccines. I know little about halfling children, but I wanted you to have Fae science on your side."

"He put a control spell on me, probably to force me to mate with Amduscias and get your precious baby for you. Have you seen how nasty your little prison has gotten since you had Warden Skinner embezzling all the money for upgrades for this plot? Do you know what kind of bacteria I could have had growing out my asshole if I had sex in there?"

"Wait a minute here, Serafina," Eiltan said.

He looked pissed off, and he had no right to be mad at my Ena after what he had done. His two black eyes and busted nose wasn't nearly enough payback for what went on in Scorchwood. He'd better tread very carefully with what he said next because while she was willing to work with him to stop Zepar, I wanted his head.

"What exactly are you talking about?" Eiltan said. "I've never been to Scorchwood. You seem to know a lot about what is going on. Perhaps more than I thought I did. I'm not going to ask how you are getting all this information because I know you neither like, nor trust me right now, but what are you talking about that Warden Skinner was embezzling?"

How did he *not* know? The paper trail on Skinner's computer led straight back to him. All the money being diverted from upgrades to Scorchwood was being funneled into investments and a corporate bank account with the name Shadow Sun Enterprises all over it.

"Ask him about Shadow Sun Enterprises, Serafina."

"What is Shadow Sun Enterprises?" she demanded.

Eiltan looked like he *really* wanted to ask her where she was getting her information. It hadn't even crossed his mind his halfling daughter would have a guardian. I wondered if it ever would. But I could see the confusion on his face. He did not understand what she was talking about.

"Something I need to look into. That's not a Sunshadow holding. We make plays on our names, but never that. We would never have a shadow eclipse the sun in an alias. It's evil luck. If I don't know about this, how do you?"

"Warden Skinner was stealing all the money meant for prison upgrades. She was barely paying the guards, and she was stealing from the food budget, so we ate the same nasty thing for three meals. All the paperwork has you as the mastermind behind all the embezzling."

Eiltan's mouth fell open, and he started stammering.

"Warden Skinner was stealing and trying to frame me? How long has this been going on?"

Serafina just laughed in his face. Really, he might be full Fae and a prince at that, but my Ena held all the cards right now. She was magnificent.

"Let me put it to you this way. Your little shithole prison had no heat, cold showers, and zero things to entertain us with. There wasn't a library to read, and we didn't even have windows to look out of. We were stuck in that icy prison with nothing to do and nothing to look at except each other. Warden Skinner staffed her guards with people she had found and blackmailed. I was framed, and so were the other elementals in this house. Are you shocked your dog bit back and framed you too?"

"You have to believe me, Serafina. I didn't know. I thought they had updated Scorchwood with modern amenities over the years. I guess that explained why Warden Skinner kept putting me off when I told her she needed cameras instead of audio surveillance. She didn't want anyone getting her hands on the tapes and seeing what the inside was like. If I knew it was that bad, I would have gotten you out of there, even if I thought you were guilty. I wasn't planning on leaving you there to rot, anyway. I hired an attorney to investigate the charges and appeal if necessary."

"I thought the Fae were supposed to be clever and make unbreakable deals? How did you manage to come up with this stupid idea and get fucked over so badly?"

"Because I fucked up, Serafina. Is that what you want to hear? I fucked up, and now the Fae may die out. I tried to make it right with no one finding out and bringing shame to my family, and I just made things even worse. Do you know how rare it is for a Fae birth now? I find out I'm a father, and everything I've done to make this right has just ended up hurting my own child. I'm sorry, Serafina. I was stupid for trying to make a deal with Zepar and was even dumber for believing Warden Skinner. I'm trying to make this right, and I know you may always hate me.

"You're smart and fierce. You wouldn't have figured all of this out if you weren't. If anyone can save the Fae and stop Zepar from taking over Hell, it's you. I know it means nothing to you, but in the brief time I've known about you, I'm proud to call you my daughter."

Insults and screaming, my Ena could handle. She was getting used to words of love from all of us, but she wasn't ready to hear that her father was proud of her. Eiltan might very well be proud of her, but he fucked up. He fucked up significantly, and it wasn't just Serafina he hurt.

She looked like she wanted to punch him again.

"Let Bael and your father deal with you. I've had enough of this," she snapped.

She stomped off to find Skoll, who still hadn't come downstairs from trying to convince the other elementals we needed to go to Hell.

Eiltan had come clean to Serafina, but it was high time he spoke to his father. He didn't want to bring dishonor to his family, but the more he tried to fix this, the worse it got. He needed to confess what he did so that the demons and the Fae could correct his mistake.

I just hoped Ior had softened towards elementals now that the Fae were having trouble conceiving. It was the law that Serafina should die. She didn't want the Fae throne. She was even uncomfortable with being a Duchess of Hell.

Surely, Ior wouldn't execute his own granddaughter. Especially when she had no intention of claiming her birthright and making trouble for him.

AMDUSCIAS

I had no idea what was going on upstairs with our elementals, but Eiltan Sunshadow pissed her off, and she had gone to join Skoll to convince them we couldn't stay here. I knew Zepar didn't offer his estate out of the kindness of his heart. As soon as we left, he would have swooped them up and tried to use them as leverage with Eiltan. If he could have grabbed Serafina without having all of Hell after him, he would have stolen her from me.

I had Eiltan Sunshadow pegged as this big, evil mastermind, but now that I was sitting in the same room as him, he reminded me of some scared little boy. Sure, maybe he really was worried about bringing dishonor to his family, but I doubted it. I saw the way his gaze followed Serafina when she stormed out. He craved her forgiveness and approval, and it was probably the same with his father.

I didn't think his father would kill his only heir for what he had done, but he would never have looked at him the same, and Eiltan knew that. He didn't want to confess his big secret until he had a solution, and that was his hubris. Eiltan Sunshadow needed as much help as he could get to fix this mess.

Hell could get Zepar's blood to cure the Fae. Zepar would die for this. Bael would torture Zepar himself. If the Fae needed his blood to heal what he did, Bael would hang him from his feet, slit his throat, and collect every drop to give to them. It wasn't just Eiltan looking bad to the Fae. Zepar made all of Hell look bad, making the Fae women barren.

It was fucked up. Eiltan grew up royalty, and Serafina grew up on the streets. Eiltan was doing everything to make sure he didn't offend daddy, and if I knew Serafina, she would not stop with that beating she gave him. She was probably still deciding if she would kill him or not. As much as I wanted Eiltan Sunshadow to pay, it sounded more like he was a man who fucked up then continued to fuck up trying to fix it. Serafina just got caught in the crosshairs.

I would not urge her to forgive him. Her feelings were legitimate, and she had every right to them. If she wanted to hate him for the rest of her life, he earned it. But I would try to talk her out of killing her father.

Eiltan deserved to be punished, but not by Serafina, even if it was her right. As a halfling, she already had a death sentence looming over her head. If she killed the only legitimate heir to the Fae throne, no matter what Eiltan's crimes were, the Fae would never let her live in peace.

I could see her grandfather possibly letting her live her life out in Hell if she was his blood and instrumental in fixing Eiltan's mistakes. Ior Sunshadow couldn't be totally unreasonable, right? It wasn't like Serafina would ever show up in the Fae realm and demand to be a princess. She could barely handle my servants waiting on her. She would be horrified with a bunch of Fae kissing her ass, and I think she would punch someone for calling her a princess, even if that was her official title.

Roman and I were awkwardly sitting with Eiltan while Serafina and Skoll dealt with a bunch of scared elementals. Eiltan had explained himself to Serafina, but he needed to explain things to me too.

"Did you have anything to do with me ending up in Scorchwood? You wanted a demon. Demons are normally turned over to Hell for justice."

Eiltan shook his head.

"I swear to you, I didn't. I'm only six hundred years old. I didn't cross the portal and make a deal with Zepar until two hundred years ago. You were already in Scorchwood. My father had nothing to do with it either. We are on the board and make decisions about the prison itself, but we don't have any say about the prisoners that end up here."

"How long has Warden Skinner been in charge? Did you appoint her?"

"She hasn't been in charge that long. The previous warden was supposed to be putting indoor plumbing in the prison. It ended up being this monumental mess. I know he got the showers in and the plumbing system, but the hot water wasn't working. The contractors he hired wanted to get out of there and didn't do a very good job. He kept insisting no one wanted to do the work. He was fired, and the entire board voted to bring Luciana Skinner in."

"She didn't fix the plumbing either. We didn't even know the showers were supposed to be hot until people started getting incarcerated that'd had hot showers."

"I never even had a hot shower until Serafina heated the water when she invited us to her shower," Roman said.

His hands were all over the place. I knew what it was. He wanted his shiv. He always played with his shiv when he was nervous in prison. Eiltan just growled at him.

"Watch it. That's my daughter you're talking about."

"Your daughter is with all of us and someone you don't see. You may or may not find out about him, depending on if she ever trusts you. You'd better get used to it because if she thinks you are judging her, she'll break your nose again. Isn't that what you wanted, anyway?"

"I wanted Serafina safe. If I had known they were all innocent, I would have gotten them out. Especially her."

"You need to call your father," I pointed out.

Eiltan ran his fingers through his blond curls.

"I can't just yet. I'm getting Luciana fired, but I can't bring this to him yet. I have to tell him about Serafina face to face, or he'll order her death. I can take care of Warden Skinner," Eiltan said, whipping out his phone.

I put my hand over his. I didn't want to touch him. It was because of him two people I loved were hurt. Maybe he didn't know about it, but I was still pissed.

"Why don't you get her fired, but tell them to let Hell take care of her punishment?"

Eiltan gulped. Yeah, we were pretty legendary in Hell for torture.

"Isn't that worse than death?"

"Man up, Fae man!" Roman grinned. "This woman framed your daughter and tried to frame you. She tortured me and let a mad warlock experiment on your daughter instead of giving her the vaccines you wanted. Don't you want her tortured?"

Eiltan went a deathly shade of white.

"The Fae don't torture."

I snorted.

"Really? We know Scorchwood started out as a Fae prison, and you locked up the Fae that didn't want to go back home," Roman said.

"How do you—how is Serafina getting this information?"

"Someone you won't find out about until she can trust you."

Just then, Skoll and Serafina came down with our elementals. I guess they were finally ready to leave. It was about time.

Bael needed to know what Zepar was doing.

SKÖLL

There were several reasons I went upstairs to talk to our elementals. Someone needed to, and Serafina needed to speak with her father instead of the elementals. Also, I was having trouble controlling my wolf. I wanted to shift and rip that fucking Fae prince's throat out for what he did to Serafina.

I had no idea what he said to her, but she came storming upstairs right as I was convincing Kestrel to come. She was the last one on board, and Serafina helped me convince her to come, even if she was clearly pissed off at her father.

Eiltan was looking at Serafina like some lost puppy when we all came back downstairs so Amduscias could open a portal to Hell. Amduscias and Roman looked a lot calmer than I felt. Maybe something was said while I was upstairs that they didn't want to kill him as much as I did.

Amduscias rarely brought us to Bael's estate without announcing us or calling first, but this time, when we jumped through the portal, we were straight in his sitting room. Bael was lounging on a sofa drinking cognac surrounded by the demons that were at Zepar's estate, and Solron was sitting at a desk glued to a laptop.

Bael bolted to his feet when he realized we had five elementals and a full Fae with us.

"Amduscias, what is the meaning of this? It was reported that all the elementals were safely at Zepar's estate. Who is this Fae?"

"Eiltan Sunshadow. He's been watching Zepar and thought he was the one that took the elementals. Zepar has betrayed us all. It's because of him this is all happening. He risks starting a war with the Fae," Amduscias said.

"The Fae still have a lot to answer for. Someone better tell me what the fuck is going on."

"The gist of it is that Eiltan Sunshadow here was on a mission from the Fae to try to make a deal with Hell for a cure for the Fae like they helped us. He took a shortcut, and instead of coming to you, he met with Zepar. Zepar gave them a remedy with his blood, and now most Fae women are barren. Zepar's help came with a call-in favor later. Zepar's favor was Eiltan sending a Fae army to overthrow the kings so he could be king of Hell.

"Eiltan had no idea what the conditions in Scorchwood were. Zepar fucked him over, and so did Warden Skinner. She's been embezzling money from the prison and making it look like Eiltan in case she got caught."

I didn't know a lot about that because I left the room, so I didn't kill Eiltan. It hadn't seemed to sink in to Bael yet that Zepar was plotting to kill him. He was still glaring at Eiltan like he wanted to maim him. Fuck, I still wanted to kill him too.

"That still doesn't excuse what was done to these six

women. You framed and experimented on your own daughter. Care to justify that to me?"

"I had no idea they were framed. I thought they were there naturally, and nothing was supposed to be done without their consent. Serafina wasn't supposed to be experimented on. She was supposed to be asked, and the only reason they took her was to give her Fae vaccines. I didn't think she knew she was a halfling, and I didn't want to put her in danger of finding out."

"Then why did you move us and lie to us? If what they say is true, you moved us and set us up with guards that were supposed to get us pregnant."

"I can answer that," Solron said. "I'm still going through the history of messages on this phone, but Eiltan thought they moved you to a better place with someone you already had a bond with. Warden Skinner was lying through her teeth."

"And you just felt the need to tell me this now?" Bael snapped.

Solron just shrugged. "I was trying to get a full picture before I made a report. Don't you always say don't speak until you have the full story?"

"You. Tell me about this deal with Zepar. I thought Fae made unbreakable deals in their favor. How did you manage to fuck this one up so badly?"

"It was my idea to approach Hell. It was my first time leaving the Fae realm. My father gave me so many lectures about not offending Hell royalty. I was so worried about fucking things up, I made a deal with Zepar and made things worse. My father has nothing but wonderful things to say about demons. I thought I could trust all of them, especially a Duke."

"Tell me everything you know about Zepar's plot."

"This was several decades ago, but he said he had three Dukes on his side and didn't have the numbers to take over Hell. He thought he could succeed with the aid of the Fae, but the Fae don't want war with Hell. We are still grateful for the land you gave us."

Bael grunted.

"You have a funny way of showing it. When you turned it into a jail for the supernatural community, you didn't cut us in on the deal. What are the names of the Dukes in league with Zepar?"

Eiltan just shook his head. "I don't have all the names. He mentioned Agares helping him once, but he didn't want to give me all the details of his plan until I had the Fae on his side."

"Does your father know what you've done, boy?" Bael snapped.

Eiltan looked more like a chastised child and less like a Fae prince.

"No, sir. I didn't want to tell him until I had a solution."

"Well, you're telling him now. We might need their help to get Zepar's blood to cure your woman. And someone bring me this Skinner woman. I'm in the mood to torture someone."

"Luciana Skinner can't just disappear tonight. She's too connected. Let me make some phone calls, and then you can take her," Eiltan said.

"You have a lot of phone calls to make, son. Ior Sunshadow needs to be made aware of what's going on. We will have to work together to fix this. And I want a new deal on the land we gave you."

"I need to go back to the Fae realm. My father deserves to hear this face to face. I'd like to take Serafina with me."

My wolf clawed to the surface. Roman hissed and bared

his fangs. Amduscias flat out told him no, but Serafina could speak for herself.

"I'm not setting foot in the Fae realm until I know I'm not getting murdered."

"When you are confessing all your sins to your father, you tell him this. Serafina is under the protection of the kings of Hell. She won't be dying because she happens to be a halfling. The Fae need to understand this if we will be working together."

"It's my condition too. The Fae will not be killing my daughter."

"Won't they just kill you too?" Roman asked.

I finally saw a little of Serafina in Eiltan when he straightened his spine and met our gazes.

"Then I'll protect her with my dying breath."

That one sentence made me want to kill him slightly less.

ROMAN

ael was pissed. Have you ever seen a pissed-off demon? A starved Vampire had nothing on Bael when he was angry. Eiltan opened a portal back to the Fae realm without Serafina. I was glad she refused to go because even if all of us didn't want her to, she'd do it anyway if she wanted to. I'd never try to control her, anyway.

We were mostly standing around awkwardly in Bael's sitting room while he paced and ranted about Zepar's betrayal. I didn't know Zepar from a hole in the ground, but I was rapidly learning a lot about him.

"That boy had every advantage growing up. He's fire born! It's not like any of us had a say on his powers or demonic form. He's always been jealous of the Dukes that are stronger than him. Just because his demonic form is a simple soldier and his powers aren't such that we could give him essential duties in Hell are no reason to act like a spoiled child!

"He should have been tortured the last time things went ass up in Hell. We didn't have any proof it was him, but we should have tortured him until he confessed. Agares too! He's another Duke that's always been jealous that his demonic form isn't intimidating. I'll bet I could fill in the other two names based on that alone!"

"What exactly is our next move?" Amduscias said. "Zepar probably had plans for the elementals. He'll realize they are missing."

"He has no reason to think we've spoken to Eiltan Sunshadow. If he asks, the elementals were uncomfortable staying there, and we moved them somewhere else."

"I can hack into Zepar's phone," Solron said. "Maybe I can get the other names."

I didn't know what hacking was, but I didn't trust these cell phones they gave us. It sounded like anyone could get into what you kept on it and read it. I was just figuring out text messages, but there were things I wanted to send to Serafina and Amduscias that I didn't want other people reading. Why was no one else questioning this?

Amduscias pulled his phone out of his back pocket and stared at it.

"Is it so easy to get into one of these things?"

Solron just snorted.

"Only if you're me. I wrote the operating system and knew how to get in. I wrote that bad boy so it's impossible to hack unless you happen to be me, and I only do it for Bael."

I had no idea what half of that meant, but even if Solron was the only one looking, I decided not to send Serafina any photos of my cock just in case Bael asked her to look at my phone. I didn't really care who saw me naked, but those photos would have been specially taken for Serafina.

"Can you do that now?" Bael asked.

"It will take a while since he's topside and it's late."

"You're right. It is. Get some sleep, Solron. Amduscias, take everyone home. The rest of you elementals, I'm sorry your first introduction to Hell has been under these circumstances, but this is only temporary. We will help clear your names so you can resume your lives topside."

"Why can't we go now?" Kestrel asked. "The Fae know we were framed and don't want us since we didn't consent."

Bael plastered this pleasant smile on his face, but did Kestrel not realize the situation she was in?

"My dear child, the world thinks you are in Scorchwood and Zepar may try to get at you. It's not safe for you until you would no longer be wanted fugitives. Hell is a perfectly lovely place once you've gotten the tour. Amduscias has a lovely palace on the beach and plenty of bedrooms for you to choose from."

Serafina took over. I could tell she was still pissed, but she always did what was needed.

"You'll love Amduscias's estate. Alozan plans the best feasts, and his servants are so nice. The beach is right there if you want to just lie in the sand and relax. The sands are pure white, and the water is crystal blue. And we'll be there to entertain you."

Pearl just shrugged.

"I'm tired, and it's been a long night. I just want to sleep. We can argue about it in the morning. Can we just go now?"

Kestrel looked like she wanted to keep arguing. Where was that fight when she first ended up in Scorchwood? The rest of the elementals shut her up when they all agreed they just wanted to sleep.

So did I. I was hungry and sleepy, and that was never good for a Vampire.

FERGUS

I didn't want to leave my Ena, knowing Hell might not be safe. But it was time to go back to the Fae realm, and she knew this. I needed to understand how Ior would react to a halfling being alive. I needed to know what his reaction was to this entire mess, but I needed to know he would not order her death.

I didn't even really want Eiltan to die. Not because he made some big fucking mistake and tried to fix it, but for Serafina. If there weren't some part of her that wanted to forgive him, she would have killed him as soon as he dragged her through that portal. She beat him to a pulp, but she stopped because she wanted to hear him out.

There was a lot we thought we knew that ended up being lies. Eiltan had made a lot of mistakes, and she had every right never to forgive him, but maybe that lost little girl from the convent who wondered who her parents were would end up eventually wanting some sort of relationship with him. I wouldn't blame her if she didn't, but I would help her if she did.

Like we portalled straight into Bael's sitting room, Eiltan went straight for his father's quarters. Ior was sleeping and bolted to a sitting position when he realized a portal was opening in his bedroom.

"Eiltan, what is it? Have you found the answer? If not, this could have waited until morning."

"I need to confess, Father. I know the reasons behind our problem and how to fix it. There are several things I need to tell you. You might want to pour yourself a drink."

Ior sighed.

"Why do I get the feeling I'm not going to like this conversation?"

"You won't. I'm just asking you to let me finish before you speak."

"I'm going to need that drink. Come to my study."

Ior poured two glasses of Nutmeg Rum and sat across from Eiltan.

"First of all, I have a child," Eiltan said. Ior looked like he was about to speak, but Eiltan cut him off. "She's a halfling, and she survived the birth without me being there to give Fae magic. She's fierce and intelligent. She would make you so proud. I don't want her killed."

"You know the law—"

"I know the law, and I don't care. Warden Skinner framed her, and she ended up at Scorchwood. In the brief time she was there, she discovered Warden Skinner has not done any of the upgrades the board voted on. She's been funneling the money into a bank account that is trying to make it look like it's us stealing the money."

"Why would Warden Skinner frame your daughter?"

"No one knew she was mine until she ended up there. I

need to tell you something, Father. The Fae are barren because of me. When I first went topside to see if Hell had a remedy, I didn't meet with the kings of Hell. I met with a Duke who wasn't in Hell.

"He promised me a remedy for a favor. His treatment did work and cure our ill, but he added his blood to it. One of his demonic gifts is to make women barren. His favor and the only way he will give us his blood again to cure our women is if we send an army to Hell to help him seize the throne.

"I brought Deaglan in. He thought if we could use the blood of a child that was mixed with demon and Fae, he could synthesize a remedy. There was already a demon in Scorchwood. When a water elemental ended up in Scorchwood, we got her consent and promised to commute her sentence if she succeeded.

"Amduscias, the demon in Hell, was utterly uninterested in her. Warden Skinner jumped the gun and just started using some money she embezzled from Scorchwood to start framing them. That was how my daughter ended up in Scorchwood.

"She convinced me to use a warlock inmate to do medical testing. She promised to keep him in line. She tortured a Vampire and conducted tests on my daughter without her consent when I just wanted her given Fae vaccines.

"She's a true Sunshadow. She broke out of Scorchwood, killing the warlock and every guard on duty. They wronged her, and she got her blood for it."

Ior cocked an eyebrow at Eiltan.

"I take it your busted face was her too."

"Oh, yes. She throws quite a punch. I knew better than to stop a Sunshadow from their revenge before I attempted to speak with her."

"You said you had an answer to our problem. We'll discuss your mistakes and your offspring in a minute. What exactly is the solution?"

"I met with the kings of Hell this time. They are angry Zepar is trying to seize the throne and was willing to start a war with the Fae to do it. I only know of three Dukes that have joined Zepar, but that was decades ago, and it could be more. Hell will get us a remedy with Zepar's blood if we help them fight if needed, and we renegotiate the contract for the real estate in Hell."

"Do you realize when it gets out Warden Skinner has been pocketing the money for the upgrades and what the conditions might be in there right now, they will shut down Scorchwood? No one will give us funding to upgrade it to make it acceptable once any of this gets out. That land is worthless for anything else. Hell can have it back."

"That's another thing. Hell wants to punish Warden Skinner for the living conditions Amduscias lived in, and Hell has claimed my daughter. They said if you order her death, you'll have to fight them for her."

"Oh, hush, Eiltan. I will not kill your daughter. With Fae births being so rare, a new Sunshadow should be celebrated, even if she's only half Fae. The fact that she survived birth without Fae magic and everything you've told me about her so far tells me she's a true Sunshadow. I'd like to meet her. We will help Hell because it means helping our people."

Eiltan rubbed his bruised chin.

"I'm afraid she doesn't have very high opinions of the Fae right now. She may punch you."

Ior threw back his head and laughed.

"Of course, she may. She's a Sunshadow. She must be a

hell of a woman if she exposed the warden, escaped Scorch-wood, and Hell is willing to fight us for her life."

"You'll be so proud of her, Father. She even looks like a Sunshadow woman. She has everything but the ears."

"I'm not going to tell anyone it was your mistake that caused our problem, Eiltan. I will tell them the demon who was mixing the remedy went rogue and did it under the king's noses to try to blackmail us. You sired your daughter on a visit to Earth, trying to hunt him down and didn't realize it. You met again when Warden Skinner framed her and experimented on her. Warden Skinner was the one who informed you that your daughter was in Scorchwood. It was the two of you and the allies she made in Hell that helped save our people."

"What about Serafina? I'd like to bring her to the Fae realm if she's willing and teach her about this side of her heritage."

"Son, I know about your aspirations of opening the portal again when you become king. I've been considering it. It's an excellent idea, and we've been closed off for too long. I say we introduce your daughter when I introduce the reopening of the portal. This time, people can bring their children back to the Fae realm if they want to. We've been relying on Earth science to help us, and now the answer lies in Hell. It's time we explore the benefits other realms can offer the Fae."

"You really mean it?"

"Yes, I do. Now, go to bed. We will go to Hell in the morning. We have to plot, and I need to meet my granddaughter."

Well, I wasn't expecting that. Ior must have gotten soft in his old age. Not only was he accepting of Serafina, he hadn't even yelled at Eiltan for what he had done. What was more shocking was that he would open the portal again. Every single Sunshadow before him had been totally against it.

My Ena was safe. If she accepted them, she would have a blood family to call her own. I knew the Fae. They weren't unreasonable when it came to halflings. If they heard about everything she had done and that she helped Eiltan with the remedy, she would have their respect.

They would probably throw an epic Fae ball in her honor that would make her horrifically uncomfortable. We just needed to clear her name, and then she would have three realms available should she want to visit or take a vacation.

She was stubborn, but I hoped she would take Eiltan up on his offer to take a tour of the Fae realm and learn more about her heritage.

SERAFINA

What a night. I was so fucking exhausted by the time we got all the elementals settled and finally fell into bed. Most of them were around my age or younger, but I didn't remember ever being that needy. I knew what they had gone through, but Clio made Amduscias's servants change the sheets before she could sleep, and Kestrel wanted softer pillows. Blossom wanted an entire bottle of wine until Alozan could call the doctor back over to prescribe her something for anxiety.

They all had some sort of demand for the servants before I could go to bed. I was so uncomfortable asking for anything I needed. I knew they didn't grow up on the streets like me, but I knew none of them had servants growing up. They were acting like now that they had access to them, they should make demands that couldn't wait. Every room in Amduscias's palace had the softest sheets I've ever slept on, but Clio wanted silk.

It felt weird going to sleep and not having anyone in my dreams. Fergus was in the Fae realm spying on my father and grandfather. It was so fucked up that my grandfather could find out he had a missing granddaughter out there and immediately decide I should die because of who my parents were.

Fergus wasn't back with me until we sat down for breakfast.

"Ena, your grandfather wants to meet you and doesn't intend to kill you. He plans on reopening the Fae portal once this mess is over. They are asking for a meeting with Bael now."

"What about Warden Skinner?"

I still hadn't forgotten that bitch framed me. I thought it was my father this entire time, but nope, it was that cunt. I would have to cut a bitch. She handpicked all of us because she thought no one would miss us. Wrong move, asshole. I might not have had anyone then, but I had people now. It puckered my butthole a little that Hell was willing to fight for me this much. Who knew? I rubbed most people the wrong way, but Hell was actually claiming me.

"Ior made a phone call before he went to bed. They've seized her bank account, but she doesn't know it. He knows Hell wants her, so they are going to let her go to work. Ior intends to let demons storm the prison and take her."

"Letting her rot in that shithole would be sweet karma."

"I think the demons have something much worse planned."

"Should I tell my family about you?"

"They may guess. There's no way you could have learned the information you did without outside help. They are on your side, my Ena. Tell them when it feels right."

"But what about us? I still want to make you real, Fergus. They don't want to kill me, but what if they want to kill you?"

"As I said, get a feel for them first and tell them if it feels right."

I hated it when he did that. I never did anything when it felt right. I got pissed off and blurted it out. I still hadn't decided if I would kill my father. I was so conflicted. He hadn't done nearly the things I thought he had to hurt me, but he had hurt me indirectly. I guess he didn't know about me, and I shouldn't hold that against him, but still, it was hard not to.

I looked out at the breakfast table.

"My father and grandfather are asking for an audience with Bael. They don't want to kill me."

Amduscias let out this huge sigh and looked at his phone.

"Then, I suppose I won't get my driving lesson. Bael will be calling soon. We still have to figure out how to stop Zepar."

"I could eat him," Roman said hopefully.

"I want to rip his throat out," Skoll growled.

"My grandfather also set things in motion for Skinner to be arrested by the demons."

"I want to torture that one personally," Amduscias said. "All of this is happening because of her."

"Are you sure we are safe here? You all sound like killers," Clio said.

"Skinner framed you and sent you to Scorchwood. It was because of her you ended up manipulated. She was lying to my father. Don't you want revenge?"

"Shouldn't she be in Scorchwood?" Pearl said.

"I say we let them torture her," Blossom said. "Klonopin withdrawals are no joke, and she put me through that just to make sure I was pregnant. Is the doctor getting here soon?"

Alozan poked her head in.

"Doctor Bogthon will be here right after breakfast. He wants to examine all of you. I'm afraid you'll have to stay here if they summon Amduscias and the others. I've asked some other elementals here to come talk to you and help entertain you."

"There are other elementals here?"

Alozan just laughed.

"Hell is not just home to demons. We have plenty of elementals here. They will be coming after your appointments to welcome you to Hell."

"They are really nice," I said. "I've met two of them. They are lovely."

We didn't have a chance to continue the conversation. Amduscias's phone rang. I'd taught him how to set a ring tone since he hated the way the phone sounded when it rang. It was totally demon of him to set his ring tone as Saint-Saëns' *Danse Macabre*. It was written after they arrested him, but he took his ring tone as serious business and went through several pieces before deciding on that one. I took a class on music in college for an elective, so I knew it well.

Danse Macabre started filling the room. Amduscias snatched his phone up and started talking.

"I want nice music when my phone rings too," Roman said. "No one ever calls me, but I still want it to."

Something just told me Roman would be into Norwegian death metal like I was. I liked other music too. Sometimes I just wanted to listen to Classical or the Beatles, but when I was stressed out, I went for the death metal.

"I want to show you some music later. You too, Skoll."

They both grinned at me. Even with everything going on and everything that had just been dumped on me, I loved showing them things about the modern world. I thought

Skoll would get a kick out of Duran Duran's *Hungry Like the Wolf* or even better, Warren Zevon's *Werewolves of London*.

I didn't realize Amduscias was trying to get my attention because I was practically making each of them a mix tape in my head. My life had gotten so fucked up since I got arrested. It wasn't the entire plot and getting framed and all that. It was the fact that I was making mix tapes for three guys in my head. I *never* did shit like that.

"We need to get to Bael's. Eiltan and his father are there and ready to plan. Bael said he's also got a bunch of antsy fairies in his sitting room wanting Serafina there."

Okay, that was fucked up too. No matter how much I had wished to meet my family when I was getting abused in the convent or getting shuffled around the foster system before I ran, I never thought it would happen. When I thought my father framed me and did all these terrible things to me, it was easy to blame him for me ending up on the street and tell myself I would kill him. Every time his eyes misted over when he looked at me, it made me so fucking uncomfortable. It would be even worse with my grandfather there.

I didn't have to tell anyone this. Skoll and Roman both pulled me into a hug. Roman did that thing I loved where he nuzzled my neck from my ear to my shoulder. Skoll cupped my ass and squeezed it.

"Just give me a sign, killer. I'll either get you out of there or rip their throats out."

I loved it when Skoll did that too. I rubbed my face into his hard chest.

"As fucked up as this makes me feel, we can't kill them just yet. We need them in case Zepar has more than three Dukes on his side now. My father royally fucked up, but he didn't set out to hurt me. He didn't get me out of Scorchwood right away because he thought I was guilty. Most of everything that happened to me was because of Warden Skinner. She didn't frame us and had Rathmore do all those things to me to help the Fae. She had her own agenda, or she wouldn't have tried to frame the Sunshadows."

Amduscias joined our hug.

"Let's get to Bael's estate. Warden Skinner is in for a rude awakening. We'll find out exactly what her agenda was. Bael is an expert at torture, and he taught me everything I know."

Amduscias opened a portal to Bael's. I knew why my father did all of this. We knew why Zepar manipulated him. Why did Warden Skinner do all the shitty things she did?

I wouldn't mind torturing her a little myself.

SERAFINA

There was an entire audience waiting for us on the other side of the portal. All the kings of Hell were waiting, but even if I had met none of these people before, I could have picked my father and grandfather out of everyone in the room. There was no question as to which of my parents I looked like now, and I used to wonder that when I was a child all the time.

We all had the same blonde curls, pointy chins, and bright green eyes. My eyes slanted upwards just like theirs did. The only different thing was that my ears weren't pointed like theirs were. They both wore their hair long and parted it around their ears like they were trying to show off the points. I was suddenly very self-conscious about my ears instead of the size of my ass.

They both stood when they saw me, and I hated how they were looking at me. As much as I had dreamed about a meeting like this, I didn't realize how much I would hate them looking at me like I was some eighth wonder of the world when I wasn't. I wasn't anything special, even if fate had decided to meddle in my life.

They both didn't make a move towards me, and for that, I was glad. I didn't like people touching me unless I liked them or had consented to a one-night stand. I was delighted they didn't get all huggy because I still wanted to punch my father again, and I hadn't decided about my grandfather. My grandfather could still order my execution by giving a single order.

My grandfather bowed his head to me. The fucking king of the Fae bowed his head to me.

"I realize you have little reason to trust the Fae with everything that has happened. If you wish to live in Hell when this is over, I wish you the best. I do hope you'll visit the Fae realm frequently and learn more about that side of your heritage."

I narrowed my eyes at him. Why was he being so kind to me? If I had been a halfling that wasn't his granddaughter, he probably would have had me killed. I knew Fergus said he would open the portal again, but would we even be having this conversation right now if we weren't related?

"Don't all the Fae want me dead because my mother was human?"

"Your father has been quite vocal about opening the portal again and letting Fae come through to try to reunite with some of their descendants. He insists allowing the halfling children to come back to our realm would further our society. He's right. The majority of my council is on his side, and the people feel the same. You would be quite welcome. This has been in the works well before I found out about you.

"The only reason I haven't given the order is that it

would be unfair to our Fae women. I worried about Fae men leaving their wives for women who could bear them children. I was planning on doing this as soon as we had an answer, and dear girl, you were responsible for bringing me the answer and exposing atrocities in Scorchwood. You are quite remarkable."

I never learned how to deal with compliments because I never got them growing up. I changed the subject because that's what I always did when anyone other than Fergus tried to give me one. I was still getting used to getting them from Skoll, Roman, and Amduscias. I didn't mind it so much from them, but it just seemed fucked up to get them now. This wasn't over. We hadn't won. We needed a plan.

"We need to save the sweet talk until this is over," I said. "Zepar will eventually figure out we are onto him. If he's recruiting topside, there's no telling how big his army is."

"We've discussed this, but it will be delicate since the Fae can't lie," Bael said. "This is all going to depend on Eiltan's ability to be cunning, and Zepar already outsmarted him once."

"Eiltan has grown up a lot since he first left our realm to cure our sickness. The only reason he hasn't taken over as king is that I made it my mission not to step down until I had a healed realm to give to him. Eiltan can handle Zepar now if you tell us your plan."

Could he? Both Zepar and Warden Skinner fucked him over. Fae couldn't lie, so how was he supposed to deceive Zepar?

"This is our plan, but it must be carried out delicately. Eiltan will contact Zepar and tell him that his operation in Scorchwood has gone ass up. There will be news stories to back this up once you make a phone call about Warden

Skinner's extracurricular activities. Eiltan will have to find a way to lie to Zepar that he will have his Fae army.

"Zepar will share the details of his attack, and the Fae army will join Zepar on the battlefield. But Hell and all its legions will also have the location and will be waiting to attack. When Zepar gives the order, the Fae will turn on Zepar and his army. Hell will join the battle and wipe them all out.

"Every soldier, Fae or demon, will have to follow orders not to wound Zepar fatally. He will have to be captured alive if we have any hope of creating a remedy for the Fae with his blood. I also want to torture that pretentious little shit for trying to take what isn't his and possibly starting a war with the Fae to do so. What he did to your women is unacceptable."

It was an excellent plan if my father actually had the ability to lie. This plan involved a lot of lying, and there was just too much at stake. Zepar wanted the Fae to attack Hell. He could do that by killing my father.

My father gave Bael this grin that made me think maybe he wasn't as inept as I thought. He looked cunning and every inch a prince at that moment.

"I can convince Zepar he has his army, even without being able to lie. He wants his army so badly, and he thinks he's worn me down into giving it to him. He's not going to ask too many questions that would require me to lie because he thinks he holds all the cards."

"My Ena, from what they have taught me as a guardian, I can help your blood too. I should be able to communicate with Eiltan the way I do with you because you are related. You can send me with Eiltan when he goes to talk with Zepar, and I can protect him. It's up to you if you want me protecting him, but

there is a lot at stake here if Zepar asks him a direct question that requires him to expose what is really going on."

"Do you mind protecting him after everything?"

"Despite all of Eiltan's mistakes, I am still Fae, and he is still my prince. This might be our only shot at stopping this. It's my duty to protect you, but if we can fix the problems in the Fae realm, we should do everything we can to do so."

"Thank you, Fergus."

"I have something to say and something that will help," I announced. "Fergus, please come out."

Fergus burst from my chest and started playing on my shoulder. Eiltan and Ior both gasped in shock. Ior was looking at me in total awe.

"That's not possible," he whispered.

"Fergus is how I found out everything I did, and he helped us escape Scorchwood."

"Do you mean you called Fergus Ó Sioráin as your guardian? He's a Fae hero. He died young, but he was a hero on the battlefield, and he died saving the king," Eiltan said.

"Yes, that's my Fergus, and he's agreed to be your guardian when you deal with Zepar, temporarily. I might as well tell you this. I'm in love with Fergus and want to wish him real. I want you to remember he helped me, and he's agreed to help you before you get all offended about how forbidden it is."

Ior and Eiltan shared this glance like they had no idea what to say to me. Ior bowed his head to me again.

"That law was written a long time ago. The fact that you managed to call a guardian at all when you are only half Fae and that you've mated with a wolf and a Vampire is telling me we are not only right to reopen the portal, but perhaps we need to revisit some of our older laws and beliefs.

"It was thought unnatural to wish a guardian real again because they already lived a full life before they died and gained the honor of becoming a guardian. I think part of that law is because it's very rare for a Fae to become a guardian when they die. Every parent wants their child to have one. I didn't get one, and neither did Eiltan. Perhaps that law was passed not because a guardian shouldn't be alive a second time, but more because if a guardian becomes real again, there are less to go around.

"Everything about you is impossible according to our laws and lore, Serafina. If Fergus felt the call and came to you, who's to say the fact that you love each other is wrong? A halfling has never called a guardian in all of our history. If Fergus is willing to protect Eiltan after everything he found out, then he clearly loves you, and who am I to say that is wrong?"

Well, fuck me. Ior and Eiltan were making it really hard to hate them. Maybe the Fae weren't all that bad. I loved Fergus, and he was Fae. Perhaps I needed to learn more about that side of my heritage.

Eiltan perked up.

"This plan of yours is good, but why go to war if we don't have to? Zepar could accidentally get killed on the battle-field, or he could realize he's losing and fall on his sword so the Fae can't get their remedy for double-crossing him. If Fergus is with me when I meet him, I could just capture him and bring him to Hell. You can get his coconspirators out of him, and the Fae can help you deal with them discreetly."

"It's a wonderful plan, but Zepar is fire born. Fergus can't hurt him," Bael said.

Amduscias cracked up laughing.

"Yes, he can. I thought I'd never get that image out of my head, but we can use it. I watched Fergus fly down a man's throat and explode him from the inside. If Fergus flies up

Zepar's nose, Eiltan can let him know if Fergus grows to his full size, Zepar will be splattered all over the walls. Or, Fergus can stay tiny, and Zepar can come quietly.

"Zepar won't think Eiltan is taking him to Hell. He knows the Fae needs him alive because his blood is the remedy. He'll think Eiltan is taking him somewhere topside to steal his blood and lock him up. He'll think once Fergus flies out his nose, he'll just portal out of there or find another way of escaping."

Eiltan looked a little green.

"Warden Skinner seemed particularly offended at the way Rathmore was killed. I take it that was the method of his execution?"

I tossed my hair over my shoulder. Was he about to get all judgey with me?

"He deserved it. He gave me a pelvic exam without my permission, put a control spell on me, and cut my birth control out of my arm."

Eiltan smiled at me like he was actually proud of me.

"You'd make a hell of a Sunshadow princess if you wanted it."

"We use both of our plans," Bael said. "Eiltan will make Zepar think he is getting his army. Get all the details you can before you unleash Fergus. Zepar will eventually break under torture and give us what we want, but knowing Zepar, he will use this opportunity to give us names of people he just doesn't like. If he's going down, he's taking his enemies with him."

We had a plan for Zepar, but Zepar wasn't the one who framed me and had Rathmore experiment on me. I knew what Zepar wanted, but what did Skinner get from all the elementals she framed?

"What's the plan for Skinner?" I demanded.

Ior gave me a huge grin. He pulled this ornate pocket watch out of his pocket.

"Everything should be handled with the board of Scorchwood by now. Press releases should be ready to go. She's sitting in her office with no knowledge of what's going on. She's ripe to disappear right about now."

Solron was bouncing happily in her chair. Bael gave her this cruel grin.

"Solron, how would you like to go play? You have my permission to knock her around a bit."

Solron jumped to her feet and looked like she'd just been given the best Christmas present ever. She opened a portal and disappeared.

I wasn't taught how to torture by a king of Hell, but I had my own questions for that witch.

AMDUSCIAS

I wouldn't usually go on a raid with a shadow demon, and I knew Solron could handle herself. I didn't care if Solron beat the shit out of Warden Skinner, but I was going because I wanted to make damned sure she ended up in someone's dungeon so I could get my chance at torturing that bitch.

Scorchwood wasn't supposed to be like that for us. Things would have been so different for Roman if those upgrades had actually been done. It wasn't his precious moon and stars, but if that rec room had been built so he'd had the illusion of being outside, he might not have hesitated when he ran and got caught. If he hadn't got caught, Rathmore wouldn't have been pissed about losing him and tortured him. Rathmore was dead, but I held Warden Skinner responsible for his torture.

I didn't want to alert Skinner with the swirling red cloud

of a demon portal. Solron wasn't mad I was coming with her. She understood why I needed to be there. We went to an unlit room with shadows. I grabbed her arm and felt the yank as we traveled by shadow to Scorchwood.

I just hoped we ended up in her office. If her office were brightly lit, we'd land in the nearest shadow. I didn't want to tip her off we were here. If she wasn't working alone, I didn't want her calling anyone.

Luckily, we found Skinner in the middle of a ritual. Her office was dark except for the candles she had lit at the corners of the pentagram she had drawn on the floor. Solron went to step out of the shadow, and I stopped her. I wanted to see what kind of a ritual the little witch was doing.

She had a secret cell phone for Eiltan in her safe and a cell phone on her desk, but she was talking to someone through magic. Several people. A coven?

"Yes, Rathmore's death has set us back. I need to replace him. It has to be another witch or warlock, and they have to be medically trained. It would take ages to give someone the same training we gave Rathmore. Is there anyone in the Coven that fits those needs?"

"That's willing to work in Scorchwood? Hardly, Luciana. Rathmore was careless and got caught. He could have exposed us all. He's lucky you got yourself chosen as warden and were able to save him so we could continue our work."

There was an entire coven of sick fucks like Magnus Rathmore? Well, they were an empire now if Skinner managed to get the cushy position as warden of Scorchwood just to stop us from killing him so he could continue his work. I needed names because they were all going down. How did this plot keep getting more fucked up?

"Well, Morgana, I can blackmail someone, but they probably won't have the stomach for it."

"Luciana, maybe it's time to stop using Scorchwood. Didn't the Fae pull the plug? If we get caught, we can't say we were doing all this for the Sunshadows anymore. You still have those women in the safe houses. Focus on them."

"Duncan, I want that halfling. It was her that ruined all of this. I still don't know how she did such a horrible thing to Rathmore, but she's strong, and we deserve revenge for what she did to Rathmore. No one kills a member of the Nightshade Circle and gets away with it. We need the demon back too."

"Face it, Luciana. Rathmore fucked up, and you fucked up. The demon is probably back in Hell where you can't get to him. If you kill the illegitimate daughter to the Fae throne, you will expose us all. Leave it."

"Fuck you, Calder. We were close. We had an entire list of test subjects that could have given us what we needed. Think of how much stronger we would have been once we had those babies and drained their blood? We would have been more than just witches and warlocks. We would have had the powers of every supernatural race. No one could stop us. We would have more respect than the elementals and the Fae."

This was still about creating the perfect supernatural even now? I had the name of several coven members and the name of the coven. I didn't want to move until she had cut off the conversation. I didn't want to tip off the rest of the Nightshade Circle that a reckoning was coming.

I hoped this was the last of the plots. Zepar used Eiltan in a plot to overthrow Hell. Skinner used Scorchwood to experiment on prisoners to gain power. Skinner was about to get taken. Zepar would end up in Bael's dungeon. The Nightshade Circle would follow.

"You're the High Priestess, Luciana, but I wish you would

listen. This will blow up in our faces just like it blew up when Rathmore was High Priest. He didn't bring the rest of us down with him. Make sure we don't go down when Eiltan Sunshadow comes for you if you hurt his daughter."

"I can handle the Fae prince. Get back to work and find me a replacement for Rathmore. Eiltan may think we have stopped trying to make a hybrid baby in Scorchwood, but that's what I want him to think."

I nodded to Solron when Skinner started blowing out candles. Our eyes were both glowing violet when we stepped out of the shadows. I hadn't shifted into my demonic form, but we were both calling on all our demonic power. Skinner started scooting back when she realized I was in her office.

"Remember me?" I growled. "The entire board is aware you've been stealing from Scorchwood and not doing the upgrades. By now, the entire supernatural community is angry with you, but you've especially pissed off some significant people in the Fae realm and Hell. It was almost a unanimous vote that Hell gets to carry out your punishment. I've got the name of your coven now too. You'll give us their names and locations after we've tortured you a bit."

"What do you want? Money? I can pay you well to let me go."

"You're broke, bitch. They froze your bank account."

"I know forbidden magic. My coven can do things for you that other witches and warlocks won't."

"Can I hit her, boss?" Solron asked.

"Yes, you can play, Solron. Just remember, she's committed crimes against three realms, and Bael wants her alive. The Fae say they don't torture, but they might want a go at her too."

I just sat there laughing like a madman as Skinner

shrieked while Solron flew at her. I kept laughing until her screams stopped. Once she was out cold, I scooped her up and threw her over my shoulder like a cut of meat.

I wasn't worried about being seen anymore, so I opened a portal and brought her straight to Bael's dungeon.

ROMAN

ell torture dungeons were something else. I was
expecting something a little more dungeon-like.
This was better digs than Scorchwood was. We
were all waiting for Amduscias and Solron to get back with
Warden Skinner, and we had no idea what was taking so
long. Eiltan and Ior had already left. Ior was gathering an
army in the Fae realm, and Eiltan was putting things in
order to snare Zepar.

I was wandering around this dungeon, wondering why
there was a bed in here. There were also sex toys like the
ones we had used on Serafina. Surely, Bael wasn't planning
on pleasuring Warden Skinner sexually. That would just be
weird. Everything about this place was strange.

Serafina was pointing at things and asking what they
were, but she avoided asking about the bed and particular
objects. Skoll just looked uncomfortable. He looked like he
would kill Bael if he said anything inappropriate to her.

We seemed to be waiting forever before a portal opened, and Amduscias and Solron hopped through. I only remembered Warden Skinner from my nightmares. I remembered her from when Rathmore tortured me, but I didn't know she was the warden until Amduscias heaved her on a slab in the dungeon.

"What took so long?" Bael asked. "I see Solron got to play, but you should have been back by now."

"Eavesdropping. Warden Skinner and Rathmore weren't working alone. They were part of a coven trying to create a perfect race. They had their own reasons for wanting a hybrid baby. I think the fact that the women had to be Dark Fae and the men pure was all her and Rathmore. They found a way to steal magic, and they planned on killing the babies. Skinner really wants to kill Serafina."

"Bitch can try," Serafina said.

"Does the Nightshade Circle ring a bell? There's an entire coven of them. I heard a few first names. There's unrest because they think she should give up on using the prison. They don't want to be exposed."

Bael just laughed.

"Oh, they will be exposed. And killed. Hell has a gigantic problem with hurting children."

I felt the same way. Who'd hurt a cute little baby just to get power? That was just gross. I really wanted to sink my fangs into Warden Skinner's neck and rip a chunk out of her carotid. Her blood smelled like it would have tasted bad, but I still wanted to kill her.

I had to resist the urge because I knew something big was coming. Bael would torture her, and Serafina had her own questions. Plus, I knew torture meant a lot to Amduscias, and I wanted to see him in his element. He was so proud of his torture dungeons. He gave us a tour of his after he popped down for sex toys, and his voice was filled with pride as he showed off all his toys. Amduscias had a bed in his too. Odd.

"Should we wake Sleeping Beauty?" Amduscias asked.

"I did a number on her," Solron bragged.

"So I see. I think you knocked out a tooth."

Bael was looking at Solron like he was turned on. Were the two of them lovers? He hadn't introduced us to any type of queen or wife. He kept Solron close during this entire investigation, and it seemed like he trusted her. It looked like he thought it was sexy that she beat the shit out of Warden Skinner.

Skinner was strapped to a table, but her scent was bothering me. Her blood didn't smell right. I needed to get closer.

"Don't wake her yet. She smells funny."

"Yeah, she's hosed down in crap perfume," Serafina said.

"No, underneath that. She's wearing the perfume to hide something," Skoll said.

So Skoll smelled it too. I was sure we looked weird standing over Warden Skinner, sniffing her beaten body chained to a slab, but it was hard to get a read on her scent with all the perfume she was wearing.

"She's more than just a witch. I know what witch smells like. She smells like a Vampire and an Earth elemental too. That shouldn't be possible."

"She smells like dirt, magic, and blood, but her blood isn't right. She's not *supposed* to be anything but a witch. Her blood has been manipulated."

"It's because the Nightshade Circle has found a way to steal magic from hybrid children," Amduscias said. "They were going to kill all the children because they needed their blood. I thought they hadn't succeeded yet, but clearly not."

Warden Skinner was an evil woman if she killed little babies. There was something about her blood, though. She'd taken the powers of a Vampire and an elemental, but it wasn't mixing well with her blood and powers. She hadn't figured out how to tap into these powers because they weren't natural.

"I don't think she can access her stolen magic."

Solron didn't hesitate. We all had to jump back as she sprayed a giant water hose on Warden Skinner.

"Well, let's wake the bitch up and ask her."

Skinner started sputtering and choking on the water. She was awake, but Solron didn't turn the hose off right away. She aimed it directly at Skinner's face so the water would go straight up her nose.

"That's enough, Solron," Bael said. "Contrary to old human beliefs, witches do drown."

Solron pouted but turned the water off.

"I was just playing with her."

"You'll get a turn. Like I could ever leave you out. You know how I love watching you work."

Yeah, those two were definitely lovers. I guess they bonded over torture. That wasn't my thing, but I would not judge them. Honestly, I was wondering if I had the stomach to sit through this. I sometimes still had nightmares from when Rathmore tortured me and what I did to people in prison when I was under his spell.

Sure, Warden Skinner probably deserved it, but that didn't mean I could sit through it with front row seats. I'd have to because I needed to be here for Serafina and Amduscias. Maybe I needed to hear what she had to say too. I lived in those shitty prison conditions, and she had Rathmore torture me. I wanted to know why. I *needed* to understand why.

I saw a different side of Bael come out as he approached the table Skinner was strapped to. He had this nasty, sharp thing in his hand.

Bael got right in her face and aimed it at her eye.

"Do you want to play nice or play rough? There's several of us here that like it rough. Oh, that's cute. Are you trying to do a spell to fight back? They ward hell dungeons against all manner of creatures. Sorry, Serafina. It's warded against you too, so you can't burn her."

"Fergus is still with me."

Bael just laughed. "Of course, he is. Not only do we not know that ward, but there's no feasible way we could capture a Fae with a guardian, no matter how cunning or strong the demon. We would have turned that person over to the Fae for justice. Plus, we've never had a Fae in one of our dungeons before."

"I'll leave the torture to the demons, but I have questions for her."

"Yes, I think every single person in this room has questions for her. Now, Luciana Skinner, how do you want to play this game?"

SERAFINA

I rarely played with my food when I brought Elemental Batwoman out to play. I collected all the evidence I needed until I was sure of their guilt before I made my move. I didn't give some great State of the Union when I killed them either. The goal was not to get caught, and getting close to someone long enough to burn them without being seen was hard enough as it was. Like I needed someone to overhear me giving this big speech about why I was killing them so they could testify against me.

But we needed answers from Warden Skinner, and it wasn't like I would feel bad if Amduscias, Bael, and Solron tortured them out of her. I lived in the prison she stole funds from instead of making it a semi-decent place. She had a warlock experiment on me and torture Roman. Not only did we need answers, but I also wouldn't mind roughing her up a bit either.

"Please, you can't do this. There are laws. I want my lawyer. Everyone gets a trial."

Bael sneered in her face.

"You committed a good bit of your crimes in Hell. This is my domain, and justice works a little differently here. You also committed crimes against the Fae who agreed to turn you over to Hell. The entire board of Scorchwood knows what you did, and your crimes are making them look bad. A long, drawn out trial would make them look even worse. They just want you to disappear. They agreed to let Hell take you too."

"The witches and warlocks won't stand for this. If I disappear, they will ask questions."

Amduscias strolled over to the table and glared down at her.

"Not all witches and warlocks are corrupt like you. When they find out what you did in Scorchwood and what you've been doing to the supernatural community, they will drop you like a hot stone. Despite all that perfume you are wearing to mask it, we know you've stolen magic from other supernaturals."

"Just kill me. You're going to do it anyway. I won't tell you a single thing."

Bael trailed the sharp object in his hand down her cheek with just enough pressure that a line of blood appeared. He got close enough to kiss her.

"That's not how things work in Hell, sweetie. You don't just die down here. We can keep you alive for years wishing you were dead. I can make it last as long as I like."

"I want to make a deal. I'll tell you everything, and you make it quick and merciful."

Every single demon in the room started laughing. Wasn't that what we wanted? We got the information, and she died for her crimes. That was how Fergus and I always worked. We got all the information we needed to help right our perp's wrong, and then we killed them. I wanted the bitch to suffer like she made everyone in Scorchwood suffer, but her death would mean it was over.

"That's not how it works here. You'll tell us one way or another. You let a Duke of Hell live in deplorable conditions. You tortured the man he loves, and you experimented on the woman he loves. That's just the tip of the iceberg. I've got five elementals here in Hell you were playing games with. All for what? More power?" Amduscias asked.

"It was groundbreaking magic and science!" Skinner hissed. "We were so close. Something about Dark Fae blood reacts well with the spell we spent centuries developing. With the right ingredients and incantation, we can use blood to transfer gifts. We just haven't figured out how to activate them once we transfer them. We thought the elementals were too far removed from their Fae ancestors. We thought we hit the jackpot when a halfling ended up in Scorchwood. It was just going to be tricky fooling Eiltan since he knew she was his daughter. We would have given him the demon hybrid, but we wanted more babies from her to test our spell on."

Now I was standing over the table sneering at her. I wanted to punch her, but Solron already did a number on her face.

"I haven't been in prison for hundreds of years. You talked about laws and wanting a trial. You still need consent for medical tests, even in prison, and you know I didn't embezzle a single dime. None of the elementals you framed were guilty, and even if they were, they shouldn't have ended up in up in Scorchwood for a white-collar crime."

"We were doing magnificent work. We would have

changed the entire supernatural community. You were a necessary casualty. You would have eventually gotten out of Scorchwood, and Rathmore would have made sure you remembered nothing if you hadn't killed him. He was a great High Priest until they arrested him. You have to be some kind of monster to kill an amazing man like that."

"Rathmore was a butcher and a baby killer. He tortured Roman. He got off light. If he had ended up in Hell, it would have been worse for him. Be glad he died quickly," Amduscias growled.

"Your little lovers and those elementals wouldn't have been harmed. We would have kept them until we got a few children out of them, then we would have let them out of Scorchwood none the wiser. I even had the other elementals moved to better facilities. If I had known you would cause so much trouble, I would have moved you somewhere that had wards everywhere."

Amduscias strolled over to a rack of torture devices and seemed to be deciding on the right one.

"She had help, you know. I killed several of those guards too, and we all destroyed Rathmore's research. We all helped."

"You destroyed nothing. Rathmore just found test subjects and made sure the women were able to get pregnant. I took over as High Priestess when he was arrested. I was the one who controlled Rathmore, and he was following my orders. I had all of his research, and I made the ultimate decision on test subjects."

Amduscias picked a pair of pliers off the wall.

"You really want to be bragging about that now? You're strapped to that slab at our mercy. Do you really want to take all the blame?"

"You're going to torture me and kill me no matter what I

say. I might as well talk about my accomplishments before I go."

"Why don't you do a little more bragging, and I won't rip off all your fingernails just yet?"

Skinner paled. She looked like she took a lot of care with her fingernails. They were long and manicured. It probably hurt like fuck to have them ripped off too.

"Did you order Roman tortured?" Amduscias demanded.

"Rathmore wanted to blow off some steam, so I allowed him when he asked me if he could. We had both decided to eliminate Jasmine's previous lovers, and Roman fell into our hands when he tried to escape. By all reports, Jasmine should have been fertile. Rathmore ran many tests on her, and she had the motive to succeed. Testing the men was much more difficult.

"We were starting to think the men were the problem. They were either shooting blanks or not willing to finish inside her so she had a chance of conceiving. We didn't want her going back or picking favorites. They were of no use to us anymore. They were lifers anyway, and no one would miss them. If they had been arrested at different times, they probably would have been sentenced to death instead of Scorchwood."

"Did you think I would fuck Jasmine just because you stuck her in my cell? The woman was repulsive, and I have standards."

"We thought you would crack eventually. Everyone in Scorchwood has sex eventually. When Jasmine seemed to fail at her task, I decided to bring more elementals in. I thought it was my lucky day finding a fire elemental I could get my hands on. I thought we lucked out finding a halfling. I was cursed the day I decided to frame that girl. None of this would be happening if I hadn't wanted a fire elemental so badly."

I threw back my head and cracked up laughing. I crawled on the table and straddled her waist. I got right up in her face.

"You really have no idea what you let into your prison when you framed me. I'm a little psycho, you know. I've never tortured anyone before, but I'm eager to see Amduscias at work. Maybe he'll teach me and let me practice on you."

Skinner tried to draw away from me, but she couldn't go anywhere.

"Get her away from me. She's crazy. I haven't forgotten the scene in Rathmore's room or the burned bodies she left behind. I don't want her torturing me. If you're going to torture me, I want it to be anyone but her."

Amduscias pulled me off the table and yanked me into a passionate kiss. He kept me pressed to his chest and scowled down at Skinner.

"It would be hugely erotic for me to watch her torture you. I'd probably whisk her back to my estate and make passionate love to her. I wouldn't even give her the chance to wash your blood off."

"Please, I'll tell you anything as long as it's not her."

"The names of everyone in your coven and who else knows what you are doing."

"No one knows outside of the Nightshade Circle, and we don't let just anyone in the coven. We have a strict vetting process because of our mission. There are twenty people in the Nightshade Circle. We haven't let a new member in since Rathmore was arrested. It was a new initiate that was responsible for his arrest. We have some parents and children in the coven, but we stopped letting children in after

Rathmore. It was the son of a high-ranking coven member that betrayed Rathmore. We couldn't take any more risks. We all could have gone down with Rathmore."

I laughed again.

"You're all going down now."

"Because of you. If I had known you were Eiltan Sunshadow's daughter and would cause so much trouble, I would have kept you as far away from my plans as possible."

"It's a little late for that now."

"You also made a grave mistake hurting Roman," Amduscias growled. "No one hurts the people I love, and Roman did nothing to deserve what you let Rathmore do to him. I will unchain your hand and you will write down the names and locations of everyone in the Nightshade Circle."

"I can't betray my coven."

"You can write those names down, or I'll slowly rip off every single one of your fingernails, then unleash Serafina on you. She's unexperienced at torture, but she is very creative. She doesn't know how to cut just right. She'd probably make a total mess with all the tools. She also likes fire and there are several things she could do to you with a white-hot iron."

Skinner had accepted she would be tortured down here and would eventually die. She didn't want to betray her coven, but she also really didn't want me to be the one to come at her on that table. I guess I made an impression in Rathmore's bedroom with all the burned warlock bits all over the room.

"I'll write all the names down as long as you don't let that crazy halfling anywhere near me."

"If any of these names don't pan out or we find out you've kept something from us, I'll unleash Serafina on you. I'll watch and enjoy every minute of it."

That was certainly new. Just the possibility of being alone with me got her to write down the names and locations of every single member of her coven. Amduscias chained her hand back up.

Solron was practically bouncing in the corner. Bael walked over and wrapped his arm around her. I thought Bael was this big, evil king of Hell and would be married to another fire born, but he never introduced us to his wife, and he seemed quite taken with Solron.

"Well, we know what scares her now. If we need Serafina again, I'll call you. Warden Skinner needs to be punished a little, so Solron and I would like some alone time with her."

Amduscias gave them a knowing smile and led us out of the dungeon to a place he could open a portal.

"Is Solron going to be the queen of Hell?"

Amduscias just laughed. "It would be quite the scandal for him to take a queen that isn't fire born, but I've never seen him so taken with a demon before. Solron is young, but she's everything he loves in women. They are probably torturing Warden Skinner together and getting off on it."

"That's fucked up in a sweet way."

"You know what else is fucked up? I got turned on watching you threaten her. I'm taking you straight to bed," Amduscias said, opening the portal back to his palace.

SERAFINA

There was so much going on. We'd started the process of stopping the witch plot, but how was Fergus going with the demon plot? I stepped through the portal into Amduscias's bedroom, and I didn't even have time to think about it. He swept me into a huge kiss and kissed me until I was panting.

"Are you mad you didn't get to torture her?" he asked.

I just shrugged.

"As long as someone is. We got what we needed."

"Somehow, I get the feeling she didn't tell us everything. She'll spill once Bael gets ahold of her. If he taught Solron, then she's good. Better than good. Solron strikes me as creative with a bit of an evil streak. She's just the right kind of demon. It's why Bael loves her. We'll have more secrets in the morning. I want you now."

I yanked my shirt off and raked my nails down his chest.

I remembered how much he loved my fingernails when I was teasing him in prison.

"Where do you want me?"

Amduscias let out a little growl and yanked me to his chest.

"Sorry, Skoll. I want Serafina and Roman in my dungeon. Do you want to watch?"

Skoll gave us this wolfish grin.

"I don't think I can watch that kind of sex. My wolf has been itching to come out since you brought Skinner back. I think I will shift and go for a run."

I broke away from Amduscias to kiss Skoll. I ran my fingers through his hair.

"Come back to me when you're done."

"Always," he said, nipping at my nose.

Skoll stripped and shifted. His enormous wolf rubbed himself against my legs. He let out a contented growl as I scratched his head. Skoll nuzzled my hand with his warm nose before bolting out the door.

When I turned around, Roman was already naked and standing there with his erection pointing at me. He had this huge, psycho grin plastered on his face.

"I was hoping we could play together soon, but I'm a little nervous about your dungeon, Amduscias."

Amduscias walked over and wrapped his arms around Roman.

"Do you want to skip it tonight?"

Roman just grinned.

"I said *a little* nervous. Not that I wanted to skip it. Let's get down there."

Amduscias kissed his forehead.

"We'll take things slow. You are both new to this, and you aren't demons. I won't be too extreme."

He opened his hand and opened a portal. I wondered why his house had hallways if he just opened a portal to the dungeon whenever he wanted to go down there. Oh, well. Maybe the dungeon was somewhere that wasn't easy to access. Bael did the same thing. Perhaps the location of Hell torture dungeons was top secret, and they didn't want anyone to know where they tortured people. I'd certainly want to keep that location a secret if I had a torture hobby in addition to arson and murder.

Amduscias's torture dungeon was in better condition than Scorchwood. No mossy walls were dripping with water, and it was a pleasant temperature in here. The dungeon was vast like it might be below his estate.

There was a section that looked deadly, but he walked us through gauzy red curtains to a more romantic area. This section had an enormous bed, an entire wall with a shelf of sex toys, and some furniture that looked like it was for play.

There was a chair on a dais that looked a little like a throne. Amduscias took a seat and stared at us with hooded eyes.

"Roman, I will take it easy on you tonight. I want you to rid Serafina of her clothes. Slowly. Make it sexy and give me a show. Kiss her and love her. Show me how much you love your mate."

Amduscias and I were both dressed, but Roman got stark naked as soon as he found out we would play in the dungeon. The lighting in the dungeon had a red tint that played well off his pale skin. His eyes started glowing red, and his fangs had been out this entire time. I wondered which Roman I would get tonight. Roman could be sweet and playful, but he also had that feral, dangerous side I loved so much. I didn't mind dancing with either of them. Amduscias was in control right now, but really, could anyone control Roman? Why would anyone want to? Roman was genuinely free now. No one should try to cage him again.

Roman stalked over to me and cupped my face. He kissed me so gently I was starting to wonder what had gotten into Roman. I felt his fang prick my tongue, and then he must have pierced his too. My blood tasted like copper after it filled my mouth, but his was different. I couldn't place it, but his blood was pleasant, and I wanted more.

I let out a little growl and deepened the kiss. Roman and I were connected on a deep level. I could always feel him now. He had full access to my thoughts and dreams. Something happened when I swallowed his blood. I could feel him even deeper. I could hear him laughing, but that wasn't possible because his tongue was in my mouth.

"It goes both ways now, Serafina. The more of my blood you have, the more of me you have access to. You're in my mind right now instead of me being in yours. You are welcome at any time. I hope you'll visit my dreams when Fergus is real, and you can touch him."

I had never wanted Roman so badly. He had this psycho side, but sometimes, he was such a teddy bear. I fell to my knees to take his cock in my mouth and heard Amduscias admonish me from his throne. What the fuck?

"On your feet, Serafina. This is my dungeon and my show. I didn't permit you to please Roman. I gave Roman an order to undress you and pleasure you."

"What if it would please me to suck Roman's cock?"

Amduscias clucked his tongue.

"I have plans for Roman's cock tonight that don't involve your mouth. Don't misbehave, or I'll spank you. See that paddle on the wall? I'll have Roman hold you down and turn your ass red."

Oh, god. If anyone else said that to me, I would have set them on fire. When Amduscias said it, it just made me curious. I wasn't in control here, and I was in control of everything in my life. Maybe I would like it if I let someone else drive for a little while. Roman was into it, and so was Amduscias. I could play this game. Maybe I would even misbehave a little because I was curious about what it would be like to have Amduscias spank me. I knew he would like to do it.

I decided to go with the flow. I'd fought against the system since I was born. I was tired of fighting. Hell was a chance to be happy, and that meant exploring unfamiliar things. I let go of Roman's cock and rose to my feet. Roman grinned at me and caressed my cheek.

"You're a little overdressed, Serafina. We have orders. We want to please Amduscias, and I want to please you."

Amduscias chuckled.

"Let's get this show on the road, but I get the feeling Serafina wants to misbehave a little."

I winked at him.

"You're telling me you don't want me to so you can spank me?"

"I'm warning you to watch it because you might not always like your punishment. Now, enough with the talk. Roman, proceed."

I wasn't dressed in another corset and skirt. Alozan managed to get me clothes that seemed to have that same steampunk vibe, but still be comfortable and easy to get into. Honestly, how they pulled that off with just a shirt and a pair of slacks was beyond me, but I fucking adored Hell fashion.

I wasn't wearing a corset, but my shirt had big metal snaps on the front. The Roman who had kissed me so gently was gone. He reached to the neck of my shirt and ripped my shirt open. He must have been in a mood I couldn't keep up with. He ripped my shirt open so hard, if there had been buttons instead of snaps, he would have ruined it. It seemed like he was in a rough mood, but he peeled the shirt off my shoulders like I was breakable.

Hell lingerie didn't disappoint. The bras were uplifting and made your girls look perky, but they didn't dig into your sides. Honestly, I would have to talk to someone in Hell about bringing this technology topside. It wasn't fair we were stuck wearing bras, and no one had figured out how to make them comfortable yet. Not in Hell. They'd figured out tit support with comfort.

"Don't ruin this bra, okay? It's quite comfortable."

Roman pounced on me. He hadn't removed my bra, but he buried his face in my cleavage. This one hooked in the front. Don't ask me how the fuck he managed to do this, but he unhooked my bra with his teeth. It snapped open, and he nuzzled my breasts with his face. I felt his fangs graze my nipple. I groaned and pulled his hair.

His hands went to the button of my slacks. He had my trousers off in seconds. He grabbed me again and kissed me until he took my breath away. I was hoping he would bite me again and let our blood mingle, but he didn't.

When he broke our kiss, he looked to Amduscias.

"I have her naked now."

"Yes," Amduscias purred. "Now, you will take her to the bed and pleasure her with your tongue. If you have her permission, you can feed from her thigh, but if you come, you had better be ready for round two because I have plans."

Roman grabbed me and practically threw me on the bed. I loved it when Roman got a little wild, and I was finding I liked it when Amduscias controlled the bedroom play. Roman was eating all of this up. He yanked my ankles apart and peered up at me from between my legs.

"Do I have your permission to bite you?"

"Roman, you don't need my permission."

He started attacking my thighs with little kisses and nips.

"Amduscias said I had to ask this time, so I'm asking."

"Yes, Roman, you have my permission."

"Now, thank her, Roman," Amduscias ordered. "Show her how grateful you are. You too, Serafina. I expect you to loudly show both of us how much you appreciate Roman's efforts to please you."

Roman was practically panting.

"Can I start now?"

"Go ahead, Roman."

There was pretty much no reining Roman in when he was like this. Sure, he was obeying Amduscias, but Amduscias just unleashed him on my pussy after building him up, and I was the one that was expected to be able to handle it.

Roman devoured my pussy. He was cupping my ass and digging his nails in. I didn't need an order to tell me to show my appreciation. I could barely stand Roman's assault with his tongue. I was shrieking and writhing like a porn star. If Amduscias wanted to watch a show, we were undoubtedly giving him one.

I was just as out of control as Roman was, especially when he slid two fingers inside me and started finger fucking me. I had enough control to turn my head and look at Amduscias. He was still dressed, lounging on his throne, and watching us with his eyes glowing that violet color again. He gave me a sly wink and a curt nod.

Right then, Roman managed to do something with his

tongue and fingers that arched my entire back off the bed. I clutched the sheets and begged him to keep doing whatever he was doing. I heard both Roman and Amduscias chuckle, but Roman didn't stop. He just doubled his efforts.

My orgasm was barreling at me. Amduscias was worried about Roman being able to go a second round, but if I came as hard as I thought I would come, I might die in this torture dungeon. Amduscias would have to finish his game without me.

Roman twisted his fingers, and I saw white. My entire body was wracked with lightning as my orgasm hit me. It only got a million times more intense when I felt Roman's fangs sink into my inner thigh. This seemed to be some never-ending orgasm. By the time it was over, I was a quivering mess on the bed, and Roman was sitting back on his heels with my blood dribbling down his chin, and a shit-eating grin on his face.

"I'm ready for the next round, but I think Serafina might need a break."

Amduscias rose from his throne and walked over to the bed.

"Yes, we will have to spoil Serafina while she recovers. Pick her up. We're going back to my bedroom for the rest of the game. I said we were starting slow, so I didn't use any serious toys. Let me grab a few things and let's get back to my bedroom."

I was one limp noodle on the bed. Roman scooped me up, and I wasn't even capable of speaking. What I really wanted was a cuddle fest and massive amounts of Chinese food.

I had a feeling if I asked, I would get it, but Amduscias had other plans for the night.

AMDUSCIAS

My first play session in my newly renovated dungeon was perfect. I wouldn't dream of breaking out anything extreme this soon. Roman was still healing from what Rathmore did to him. I'd never traumatize Roman. I wanted to help him heal. I wanted Roman to feel free here. To do that, I just gave him a little guidance to deepen his bond with Serafina.

At his heart, Roman enjoyed pleasing people. He was a total wild card, and I could never predict what his mood would be, but there was always something deeply Roman that I could always count on. Despite his history of murdering inmates, which was beyond his control, Roman wanted everyone around him to be happy. That was pretty fucking hard in Scorchwood, and that was part of why Roman went so crazy in there.

I also wanted to please Roman. I had so many plans tonight, but I also wanted to spoil Serafina. I love that girl too, and I would make damned sure she was spoiled rotten here in Hell. That convent that mistreated her and life on the street would be a thing of the past.

I had both of them to take care of tonight. I knew Roman would get off on pleasuring her, and I just wanted to listen to the little noises she made when she was feeling good. Roman had done a number on her. She had this dazed look on her face when he gently set her on the bed.

We both snuggled into her and just held her.

"What do you need, Serafina?"

"Can you get Chinese food in Hell? It's my favorite, and I'm starving."

I'd move mountains to get this food in Hell if we didn't have it. I grabbed my phone. I was still getting used to phone calls and text messages, but it was certainly a handy device. I texted Alozan to ask. Apparently, we had plenty of Chinese food in Hell, and someone would drive it to us if we wanted. Excellent. I could feed Serafina her favorite food in bed.

"Alozan said there's an app we can order it from, and they will bring it to us. There are several places to order from, but I'm afraid you'll have to order for me."

"Me too," Roman said.

"I'll order a feast, and we can share. That's the best way to eat Chinese food."

She perked up a little as she scrolled through the app and picked out a meal for us. I didn't mind taking a brief break from my game so she and Roman could eat. Honestly, this was my first time playing in hundreds of years, and I would go all out. I'd probably keep them up all night. I intended to do a lot of playing, but I also planned on spoiling both of them. I wanted to spoil both of them for the rest of our lives.

We snuggled until the food came. Honestly, I could have

snuggled both of them for the rest of the night and been happy, but I needed to prove a few things to myself. They had locked me up so long, I needed to know I could still do this and who better to find that out with?

Alozan brought the food up, and honestly, it was so much fun sharing food with them. It wasn't served on fine china. It was in paper containers, and we ate it with plastic forks and strange sticks. I got to share her favorite food with her and decided I liked it enough to explore the cuisine more.

She lit up as we ate and shared food, and what's more, so did Roman. We all needed this. I just wished Skoll could be here. I wasn't interested in Skoll romantically, but I knew he lived for her smiles, and we were getting a lot of them right now.

She set her container of food down and rubbed her belly.

"Now that my stomach is full and my body has stopped shaking, I believe you mentioned a round two."

Roman started bouncing. He always had this frenetic energy when he got excited. He was like this hulking, angelic-looking child. His entire face would light up, and he would have trouble sitting still. I loved it when he got this excited about something because I didn't see it often in Scorchwood.

I broke into a grin.

"Roman pleased you, and we've shared you. Now, we will share Roman."

Serafina immediately perked up and started stroking Roman's arm.

"Oh, I was hoping we would eventually do that. Roman is precious to me. I want him to feel as special as I felt when all of you were sharing me."

Roman stopped bouncing and looked utterly embarrassed. The Vampire had no problems stripping naked at the mere mention of sex in my dungeon. He was naked now, but he was uncomfortable at sweet words. I realized after being cooped up in Scorchwood for so long, Serafina wasn't the only one I needed to be whispering sweet words to. Roman needed to hear them too.

I started playing with his hair.

"You're special to both of us. Let us show you."

"How?"

"You're going to make love to Serafina while I make love to you."

"We will make a Roman sandwich," Serafina said.

Roman was still looking shyly at his hands, but his cock was rising to attention.

"It's strange, you know. Being here after being locked up for so long. I'm surrounded by people I love. I don't want to mess this up."

"You're my mate, Roman. I'm not going anywhere."

"I didn't leave in Scorchwood. I will not leave now that we finally have the chance to be happy."

Roman finally met my eyes and grinned.

"Yeah, you didn't leave me. You could have walked out at any time."

"And I'm not leaving now. What do you want, Roman? Do you want to talk, or do you want to play?"

His mood changed in an instant as it was prone to do. His eyes flashed red, and he was back to bouncing.

"Let's play. I'm curious."

Serafina just smirked at me. She knew it was game on.

"You're the game master. Tell us how you want to play this."

I didn't leave my dungeon empty-handed. I was quite

fond of all the sex toys that had been developed since I got arrested. The lube was so much nicer, and there was an entire array of toys to make anal sex so much easier. I hadn't begun to explore all my new toys, but I'd used several of the anal toys on Serafina, and I quite enjoyed the noises she made when I used the vibrating toys on her. Now, I wanted to see what those toys could do on a man.

"Roman, I want you to stand in the center of the room. Bend over and brace your arms on the table. Serafina, you will get on your knees and return the favor Roman gave you in my dungeon, but you aren't allowed to make him come. I need to prepare him."

They did exactly what I asked, and Serafina on her knees, licking Roman's cock, was quite the sight. Roman's face was sheer pleasure, and she wasn't just sucking his cock. She was putting on a show for me. My cock stiffened to the point of pain as I stood watching.

I shook myself from my reverie. I had a job to do. What we were about to do would be pleasurable for all of us. Serafina would feel Roman thrusting into her and me thrusting into Roman. Roman would have double stimulation. My cock would get pleasure too, but I could also go to bed knowing Serafina and Roman both felt special tonight. That was what made it all worth it.

I walked behind Roman. He really did have a beautiful body. He was pale like all Vampires were, but his skin was getting a lovely rose tint from regular feeding and fresh air. His body was beautiful and muscular. He had the ass of a male ballet dancer.

I ran my hands over this firm, round ass, then gave it a hard squeeze. Roman let out this huge moan. His moans only got deeper and more passionate after I squirted lube on his ass and started fucking him with my fingers. I thought about this so much in Scorchwood, but I never thought it would happen.

I took my time fucking his ass with my fingers. I wanted this to feel as good for him as possible. It wasn't like either of us had done this in hundreds of years. When I thought he was ready, I stopped. Roman groaned like it disappointed him when I removed my fingers. I would have kept going, but I had other plans.

I gave Roman a light tap on the ass.

"Step back and stand by the bed. Serafina, go lie on the very foot of the bed."

"Yes, sir," she said, saluting me.

She had no idea she'd be calling me sir in the inevitable future. She would challenge me. I had a feeling she would enjoy being punished and misbehave just to end up in my dungeon. And I had no problem with that at all.

Serafina sprawled on the bed and spread her legs. Her eyes bore into Roman as she fingered her clit. She crooked her finger at him, beckoning him to come close. Roman was back in a playful mood and went scrambling over.

I swatted at his ass as he streaked past me to get to her.

"Get that cock in Serafina, Roman."

I didn't have to tell that Vampire twice. He was buried inside her before I could blink. Now, that taut little ass was just waiting for me. I oiled my cock up and positioned myself behind him. I eased into him gently and slowly. Roman stayed still with his face buried in Serafina's neck. I could hear his muffled moans of pleasure.

When my hips met his ass, I petted his back fondly.

"How are you, Roman?"

"Amazing," he sighed.

"Then, make love to your mate while I make love to you."

Roman began to move, so I did too. I let Roman set the pace. I'd shared Serafina with Roman, and I knew he liked things a little intense when he was making love to her. I liked to drag things out, but I was doing something different tonight.

I pounded Roman's ass. I had a lovely view of Serafina's face over his shoulder, and her nails raking down his back. I was definitely going to have to make a date with her where she scratched me up. The room was full of her cries, Roman's groans, and my moans.

This was better than I ever imagined. I couldn't even begin to hold Roman still. I was gripping his hips, but the Vampire fucked like a wild man. I went a little out of control too. I knew when Serafina came. I'd long learned the noise she made when she did that. Her nails drew blood down Roman's back. Yeah, I definitely wanted to feel her nails draw blood on mine.

Roman flat out threw back his head and bellowed when he came. I could finally let go. I pounded his ass harder until I came. I came hard too. I would leave fingerprints on Roman because I was grabbing his waist so hard. I sighed as my cock released all the pressure that had been building.

It was fucking amazing. It was better than I could have imagined. Now, I just wanted to hold them and tell them how special they were. I pulled out of Roman.

"Now, we snuggle," I ordered.

Serafina and Roman shakily crawled to the head of the bed. I snuggled into Serafina and pulled her to me. We might have just shared Roman, but Roman and I were both holding Serafina. With the sleeping arrangements, we never got to hold her at the same time.

She kissed Roman, and then she kissed me.

"The two of you are amazing. You've become quite special to me. I don't want this to end either."

I squeezed her.

"I could never leave either of you."

"That's not what I'm worried about. We still have to deal with Zepar. I want to make a home here, and Zepar intends to bring war. Fergus is with my father, so we can't talk and get updates."

Ah, yes. I didn't want to talk about Zepar right now. I just kissed the tip of her nose.

"The demons and the Fae are working to bring Zepar down. I wouldn't worry about him."

I didn't care if I had to hunt him down and do it myself. Zepar would die.

FERGUS

I volunteered for this, and I knew why it was needed, but it was killing me being away from my Ena. I stayed close to Eiltan, but I kept reaching through my bond with her to check on her. She was safe and happy. I knew she always would be around Skoll, Roman, and Amduscias, but there were enemies in Hell.

I didn't think I would ever see Ior Sunshadow in a hotel room on Earth, but there he was. It was a penthouse suite, of course. Only the best for the Sunshadows. They hadn't made a move on Zepar yet. Eiltan knew where he was. He wasn't totally hopeless, despite all his fuckups. He'd been monitoring Zepar's movements. The only reason he hadn't made a move and sent a Fae army to take him was that he didn't want to start a war with Hell.

That minor impediment was off the table. Hell wanted Zepar just as much as Eiltan did. They had every reason to get the Fae his blood. I'd been a guardian for a very long time. I'd watched the Fae grow and evolve. One thing had never changed. You didn't conduct a lousy deal. Sure, most deals swung in the Fae's favor, but they were always fair.

No Fae would ever resort to what Zepar did to turn a deal to their favor. It would be considered dishonorable. Eiltan didn't even think Zepar would betray him when he left their deal open-ended because that just wasn't how deals were done. I still wanted to throttle him for not thinking it could be a possibility. Still, I wasn't throwing all the faults on him. He was a young Fae, and he had only just started taking his princely duties seriously. Ior should have sent someone more experienced with him.

I had just been sitting there listening to Ior and Eiltan plan. Everything I knew about Ior was that he viewed Eiltan as a disappointment, but now I knew that was a lie. Ior really loved his son. He wanted this to end in a way that Eiltan came out the hero and it wasn't just to make the Sunshadow name look good.

They were plotting how to get him in Hell. They weren't asking my input much because neither of them was used to having a guardian at their disposal.

"Won't he think it's a trick if you ask to meet after all this time? You say you've only spoken to him on cell phones since they were invented."

"It'll be perfect, father. Zepar thinks he's won. He thinks everything I tried to get around him is blowing up in my face. He thinks my daughter is in Hell right where he can get to her when he wants. Zepar will think I have nothing left to lose, so I'm finally giving him an army."

"I still think I should be there when you meet him. It'll make more sense that we are negotiating war with Hell with the king of the Fae there."

I finally decided to chime in. They'd probably forgotten

I was there, but I didn't mind. I was Serafina's guardian, not Eiltan or Ior's. I was just here to help.

"I've met Zepar too. He has an ego. It's why he wants to be king of Hell. It's not that he thinks he can run things better. He wants to be adored. It will trip him up if the king of the Fae met with him in person. Everyone knows you stay in the Fae realm and send ambassadors when you need something outside of your kingdom.

"Zepar's weakness is his ego. We can get his guard down by having Ior appear in person, and I can fly into his nose or mouth. I wouldn't trust him even with me resting in his lungs or stomach. If you have warded handcuffs, I would get them on him before he can open a portal. He doesn't know Serafina has a guardian. Bael kept that on a need to know basis when we got to Hell. He may know a guardian ward. If he gets one tattooed on his body, it would expel me. Fire can't burn him, so he's not going to have a ward up for you. He won't have a guardian ward up because he thinks neither of you has them. I need to come out at just the right moment, and then you need to get demon warded handcuffs on him so he can't open a portal."

"I have all sorts of demon warded items, but when we used to meet in person, it was always in a human-run hotel. That way, it wasn't warded against demon or Fae. Zepar knows I won't set foot in one of his businesses, and he's not dumb enough to meet in one of mine. We both brought a bodyguard who frisked us before we went in. Getting handcuffs in would be very difficult, but not impossible."

"How exactly would you sneak demon warded handcuffs into a hotel room with all the precautions you both take? If you can get those in, couldn't Zepar sneak a ward in?"

Good question. I had disliked and distrusted Zepar almost on sight. It was before I knew he tricked Eiltan and hurt the Fae. I didn't like the way he looked at my Ena, and I didn't think he should have been at that meeting with the other kings. I knew why he had inserted himself now. It made sense, though. If Eiltan could sneak something in, Zepar could too.

Eiltan just grinned.

"Quite easily. Zepar is rude to everyone he deals with. He might be polite in Hell because there are more powerful people down there, but he considers himself superior on Earth. Everyone he works with hates him. He treats the employees of every establishment he goes to like garbage.

"The human hotel we always meet at is one we use often. I would wager the entire staff hates him. I treat them all with respect, and I'm a good tipper. I have a beneficial relationship with the managers there. They've banned him from the hotel many times for his behavior, but he knows the CEO of the hotel. He just calls and complains. The hotel managers get berated and have to allow him back. All I have to do is promise them if they leave a bag under the mattress, I can make sure Zepar never visits their motel again, and I would be doing nothing illegal in their hotel."

"You still have to get the bag to your manager friend without tipping Zepar off."

"While Zepar was making enemies, I was making friends. I've got demon warded weapons stashed with sympathetic covens all over the country. All I have to do is make two phone calls, and a witch or warlock will bring the bags to Logan to stick under the mattress."

"It's not going to be so easy. Even with his guard down because he thinks he's won, Zepar has fooled the kings of Hell for centuries into thinking he doesn't want their throne. My advice would be to move fast. He will pause when he realizes he's got a

Fae guardian inside him that can make him explode. He's going to need a minute to think of a way out of it.

"He knows I'm only going to react as a last resort because you need his blood. His first reaction, once he's realized what has happened to him, will be to portal away to regroup. You'll only have seconds to get those handcuffs on him and neutralize him," I said.

Eiltan laughed.

"Let's just say Zepar pissed off this coven. They've come up with their own ways of neutralizing him if I needed it. Zepar won't discuss business until he's had his favorite scotch. Sakura is the High Priestess. The Hallowed Guide Coven are healers. They were also looking into a potion that would heal the Fae. They concocted one that should make the scotch hit Zepar harder. He'll be disoriented and confused when Fergus comes out, and we should be able to get the handcuffs on him."

Zepar had an ego, but so did the Sunshadows. I wasn't ashamed to admit my own people could be arrogant. Just like we could use Zepar's ego against him, Eiltan and Ior needed to rein theirs in because anything could go wrong. Zepar could have friends, and he sure had people who did his bidding because they were afraid of him. And if Warden Skinner had taught us anything, people were willing to commit all kinds of atrocities for enough money or if you had enough dirt on them.

"Use everything in your arsenal, but be prepared for Zepar doing the same. He deceived you once, and he's tricked everyone in Hell. Don't go in there thinking you've already won or you'll tip Zepar off."

This was a delicate operation, and we didn't need three raging egos in the room, all thinking they had won before they even set foot in that hotel room. That was a disaster not even a guardian could fix.

FERGUS

E iltan tried to get his ducks in a row before he called Zepar. The rest of the world must have disliked Zepar as much as I did because everyone Eiltan called was willing to fuck him over if it meant getting rid of him. His witch friends were ready to deliver the handcuffs and a magically roofied bottle of Zepar's favorite scotch to the hotel. The hotel manager was willing to slip the bag in a desk drawer in the sitting room and have room service deliver that specific bottle of Scotch.

Zepar had pissed that High Priestess off so much she wanted to book the hotel room next door and have the entire coven waiting in case something went wrong. Honestly, that wasn't a terrible idea, but the hotel room couldn't be right next door. Zepar would sense that many witches and warlocks in the next room. They needed to be close enough to come if needed, but not close enough for Zepar to detect them.

Serafina was stubborn, but at least she always had an open ear to suggestions and was willing to talk things out. She certainly didn't get that from her father or grandfather. Eiltan and Ior both thought their way was the best way. It was like they didn't want my wisdom as a guardian. They just wanted me to come out at the last minute so they could threaten Zepar with me. It was infuriating.

"Listen, I am older than both of you put together. I've fought in wars before. I've guided several Fae, and the only reason Serafina was able to stay hidden for so long was because of me. I didn't agree to come here with you just to threaten Zepar with me. I came to give you the same guidance I give your daughter."

"He's right," Ior said. "We need to be listening to him. Fergus, I'm sorry. Neither of us is used to having a guardian. We are used to bouncing opinions off each other or advisors. What do you think we should do?"

"I think you should fill all the rooms close to your meeting room with all the allies you can call, but put them far enough away that Zepar can't sense them, and don't put them in the hall leading to the room. As he walks to the room, he can't sense there's an army of supernaturals gathered in that room.

"The witches need to spell a mirror in the room so that everyone can watch and see if something goes wrong and respond immediately without you whipping out your cell phone and making phone calls. You also need to be prepared for the fact that Zepar may sense we have drugged his scotch and try to portal out of there before I can get to him and you can get those handcuffs. If there's any other advantage you can think of, you should use it."

Ior stroked his beard.

"Would your hotel manager friend let the witch put a demon ward in the room if we promised to remove it? If she puts it behind the mirror, he won't see it."

"He need not see it. You can't ward the room. He will scan the room for wards before he goes in. I don't think he'll be looking for warded objects. The two of you have never had Fae wards used against you before, but I have, pretty recently, in Scorchwood. You don't have to see them. You can feel them if you check for them, and I don't think Zepar will go into that room without checking."

"He's right, Father. I check for wards too. I didn't trust that Zepar would try to abduct me and ransom me for his army."

"Well, what other advantages can we use?"

"I made allies with the shifters, and they taught me other ways to fight. Ways Zepar wouldn't know. Zepar's demonic form is a soldier in armor. It's not like some other demons. It's just a man, not a beast. I've never seen his demonic form, but I'm much bigger than he is, and I've wanted to beat him since he swindled me.

"Once the scotch kicks in, I'll pretend to check on him like I'm concerned. Once I get close enough, that should be when Fergus comes out. I'll be right next to Zepar in case he thinks about opening a portal. I can grab him while Father gets the handcuffs. If he tries to fight, I can knock him around a bit. He has it coming."

That was actually an excellent plan. I had no idea how Eiltan managed to find out Zepar's demonic form when Amduscias was so secretive about his until it was needed. We didn't start learning Hell secrets until we got to Hell, so I had no idea how Eiltan was getting some of his information.

"It's a solid plan, Eiltan, but call for backup."

"I agree, son. Call your allies, then call Zepar."

I hoped this meeting with Zepar happened soon. I hoped we got him to Hell and could squash his little rebellion. The fate of the Fae lies in us taking him alive, and it was killing me being away from my Ena.

FERGUS

Eiltan gathered enough allies to fill half the entire floor of the hotel room. He put the phone on speaker when he called Zepar. He was feigning defeat and promised a meeting with his father to get Zepar his army. That slimy demon's voice was dripping with so much arrogance, it made me want to ruin this entire plan and make him explode when I flew down his throat.

Zepar didn't want to dally, but Eiltan had clearly grown a lot since the first time Zepar deceived him. We all knew Zepar would not discuss business at the hotel until he savored the moment with his favorite scotch. He would not be able to do much talking once the witch potion kicked in, and we would be moving fast to get him to Hell.

None of us were stupid. I didn't even have to tell Eiltan and Ior to see if they could get Zepar to spill as much as they could over the phone. He certainly wasn't going to in Hell. At least, not right away. He would keep his mouth shut, hoping his allies came to rescue him when they found out he was taken.

I was pretty damned proud of Eiltan as he worked Zepar over the phone. I saw a little of Serafina.

"My father has promised his army, but we need to know we can win this. The Fae still have a military, but we haven't had a war in centuries. It's not as big as it would be if war was brewing. Do you have enough demon support?"

Finally, Zepar didn't sound like he had already won. He had the gall to sound offended.

"Well, it's not like I can just go bringing something like that up at dinners. Many people in Hell are loyal to the seven kings, and I know better than to ask them. I've got three Dukes and all their legions on my side. I had much better luck topside. There are plenty of supernatural mercenaries from all the groups. They don't care who they kill as long as you pay them enough.

"I'm a billionaire on Earth with the business I've built for myself. I've promised them all favors or money. I've handpicked seven of the top assassins in the world. I have a plan. I will sneak them into Hell. They will infiltrate each king's palace and kill them. Our armies will swoop in during the chaos and make sure I seize the throne. I think there will be so much chaos, not a lot of lives on our side will be lost."

"I want the cure you promised. You get your army, and we get the cure."

"I'm a demon of my word. I can't be known as a king who dishonors deals. My first act as king will be to cure your women. I want a beneficial working relationship with the Fae once I'm the king."

I was glad I was invisible because I was laughing out loud. Zepar may have been able to outsmart a young, inexperienced Fae, but he was clearly the dumbest demon in all the realms if they thought the Fae would let this slide. I wouldn't be shocked if Ior got his hands dirty torturing Zepar himself. When Ior and Eiltan went back to the Fae realm with the cure, our people would want to hear that Zepar died for what he did. They would want to know everyone that helped him was dead too.

Zepar was delusional. He thought he could take Hell with three Dukes and an army of mercenaries and Fae. I'm sure his assassins were quite competent, and Zepar knew the layout of all the king's houses. Zepar's demonic form might be a soldier, but I'd seen Amduscias's unicorn. I'd seen the damage he did. If Amduscias was a Duke and not a king, I could only imagine Bael and the other kings had demonic forms that could take on an Earth assassin.

"I'm not king yet, Zepar. You will have to work all that out when you meet my father tomorrow. I know there are things in Hell he wants. Maybe you could broker a trade deal."

"I want to meet as soon as possible. Tomorrow morning at eight. The same hotel as usual. Bring your father. We have many things to discuss."

Eiltan hung up the phone. I knew I promised to stay and help, but Hell needed to know what Zepar said.

"I'm going back to Serafina to check in on her and let her know what Zepar said. Amduscias can relay the message to Bael."

"Yes, go. And make sure she's happy and safe," Eiltan said.

What exactly did he think I did as her guardian?

SERAFINA

It was so fucked up. There was a demon intent on conquering Hell and the witch who framed me in a torture dungeon, but no one needed Elemental Batwoman. If there was any time for all the hobbies I'd perfected, wasn't it now? Fergus was off kidnapping demons without me, and no one wanted my help with the evil bitch who was framing people and experimenting on them unless their methods didn't work. She feared me. Shouldn't I be down there with them? I just felt useless.

I didn't want to fuck, and I didn't want to watch TV. I wanted to be out there ending this. I was going crazy. It felt like I'd spent my entire twenties murdering people and burning shit down, preparing for this moment, and now I'd been sidelined.

The guys knew I was antsy and were trying to help.

"Do you want to go back to Bael's? He promised her he would only unleash you if he thought she was lying, but I'm sure he would like it if you threatened her to get information out of her," Amduscias said.

"Maybe. It feels like I should be doing more than just threatening people."

Amduscias pulled me into a hug.

"He made a promise to Warden Skinner, but I'm sure he'd let you knock Zepar around a little when he gets here."

"It feels like I should be with Fergus bringing Zepar down here. We *always* work together. I know why he's helping my father, but something doesn't feel right about this."

"Is it because you don't trust your father?" Skoll asked.

"Fergus is an ancient Fae guardian, but he doesn't perform miracles. Zepar already deceived him once, and so did Warden Skinner. How do we know Zepar won't be the one doing the kidnapping? If he ransoms a Fae prince, he may get his Fae army."

"Ena? I have news."

"Fergus is checking in!"

"Your father was brilliant. He knows all of Zepar's secrets and weaknesses. We have a plan to take Zepar that I'm almost certain will work. What's more, when your father called him to set up his meeting, we found out some of his plans. He has three Dukes on his side, but he mostly recruited on Earth. He has mercenaries, and he hired seven assassins he would sneak into Hell to take care of the kings. He would not show up with his armies until his assassins had taken care of the kings."

"You think you can take him and nothing goes wrong?"

"Something can always go wrong, my Ena, but I think we can pull this off."

"Thanks, Fergus. I'll get the message to Bael. Come back to me soon."

"I miss you, my Ena."

I relayed everything to Amduscias. He didn't hesitate, and he didn't call first like he usually did. He opened a portal straight to Bael's dungeon. Bael and Solron were still down there with Warden Skinner, who was now naked and covered in blood. Solron was hovered over her with a scalpel and scowled when she saw us.

"Wait your turn," she snapped.

"We aren't here to torture the witch. Fergus checked in, and Eiltan found out Zepar's plans. He's got assassins picked for all seven kings. He's probably shared with them the best way to get into your estate and what he thinks is the best way to kill you."

"Which demon assassins has he recruited?" Bael roared.

Amduscias cleared his throat.

"He did most of his recruiting topside. They aren't demons. I think he knew almost all the demons here are loyal to the kings, so he extorted the Fae and paid people topside."

Bael sighed.

"Intelligence never was one of his strong points. If he hadn't been fire born, he'd probably be cleaning my toilets. I'm shocked he's been so successful topside. The only reason we agreed to let him go was that we thought it would teach him a lesson. Instead, he had some success and tried to make himself king of Hell."

"He's gotten pretty far with his plot," I pointed out. "What are you going to do with him if they manage to get him down here?"

"If? Do you doubt your guardian, girl?" Bael asked.

I loathed when men called me that, but it wasn't like I could punch the king of Hell in the face without offending someone.

"This entire plot depends on several people, not just

Fergus. Fergus just met my father. He can't anticipate his moves like he does with me. Ior will be there. If either of them slips up, Zepar could portal away before Fergus makes his move. Fergus can't exactly talk to him if Zepar gets away with Fergus in his stomach, and Fergus says if he gets a guardian ward tattooed on his body, he would be expelled. There's a lot to chance. Fergus can't kill him if he gets away, or we lose our cure for the Fae."

Bael put his hand on my shoulder.

"I spoke with both your father and grandfather after you left. Eiltan has grown up a lot since Zepar first deceived him. I know he made mistakes looking for the cure for his people, but while he was looking, he managed to find out things about Zepar that only Hell would know. He had several ideas before he left. If he had a Fae guardian helping him once he left, I'm sure the plan is perfected, and Zepar will replace Skinner on my table."

"Have we learned anything else from the witch?" Amduscias said.

Solron aimed the scalpel right at her eye.

"Nothing useful. Anything you would like to confess, witch?"

"Did you say Zepar? My coven knows him. We do business with him."

Okay, well clearly she would confess something, but I hadn't forgotten that bitch framed me and made everyone in Scorchwood live in deplorable conditions. Maybe Elemental Batwoman could play a little. I walked over to the table and looked at Solron.

"May I?"

Solron lowered her scalpel and pouted.

"Oh, go ahead. I've been playing with her for hours."

I climbed back on the table and straddled her waist. I

was getting blood all over my nice new jeans, and I didn't care. Solron didn't care about not marking her face up when she was doing her cutting. I didn't get too close to her face because I didn't want blood in my mouth. I had no idea if she was carrying something I didn't want to catch.

"Tell me about your dealings with Zepar. Tell me everything, or I'll go a little crazy on you."

"Zepar knew what our coven mission was. He knew Scorchwood used to be a Fae prison. He also knew I managed to get myself assigned warden to make sure Rathmore wasn't murdered. It was Zepar that suggested using inmates as a means of not getting caught like Rathmore was. He became one of my outside consultants. In exchange for his advice, we would do forbidden magic for him. He dealt with Rathmore before, and then I took over after they arrested him. All Zepar wanted from us was large and frequent supplies of persuasion potions."

"Well, that answers how his business was so successful," Bael muttered.

"Was it Zepar that suggested framing the Sunshadows for your embezzlement?" I asked.

"He didn't know it was them. He suggested taking the money to fund our research, but he suggested framing either someone that works at the prison or a board member. I never told him it was Eiltan because he always had this weird obsession with the Fae. He would have been angry if he knew the paper trail pointed to Eiltan."

"Then, why do it?" I growled.

"Because even if Zepar was giving us excellent advice, he was an asshole. Some of his advice was straight up useless, and he was rude to my coven when he picked up his potion. Once you start doing anything with Zepar, there's no way out. Anyone who has tried has ended up dead. He's like this one-person demon mafia. I knew Zepar was obsessed with Eiltan Sunshadow, so I tried to frame him to get back at Zepar."

I laughed in her face.

"You're a passive-aggressive bitch. Do you know that? Did you tell Zepar you had his daughter in your jail?"

"Of course not. I had plans for you. If I had known keeping you in my jail would end up with me on this table, I would have, though. I would have told him to take you anywhere but my jail."

Warden Skinner absolutely *loathed* me like I was the one who had done wrong here. Sure, I killed her friend and every guard on duty, and sure, it was because of me she was down here getting tortured, but she was the one that fucking started it. I wasn't the one going around framing people and experimenting on them. I just made sure she got caught. She could hate me all she wanted.

"Let's take a break, Solron. Serafina, get off the warden," Bael said. "We need to prepare for the morning. If everything goes our way, Zepar will be in my dungeon, and we can play with him too."

I guess I was going back home. I had three guys to keep me occupied until morning. I desperately missed Fergus, but I should be reunited with him in the morning. It didn't feel right to be having sex right now.

I decided to teach the guys to drive. I could go for some good old-fashioned road rage right about now.

FERGUS

It was time. I hadn't realized how much went into these meetings. Zepar was waiting at the hotel bar. He was already enjoying a glass of scotch. Eiltan approached him with Ior and made introductions. If you ask me, Zepar didn't show the proper reverence for meeting a Fae king. He was only a Duke. He should have groveled more.

They walked together to the front desk to collect the key. It was like neither of them could have the key first to get to the room before the other. The manager escorted them to their room and showed them inside. He gave them both a curt nod.

"I'll send room service with your bottle of scotch and a cheese tray."

Zepar grinned. "Send a full meal. We'll be in here a while."

We wouldn't, but let him think that. Room service came almost as soon as the manager shut the room. Things were moving quickly. Zepar poured his scotch. I wondered how Eiltan would get out of drinking it if he proposed a toast. I hadn't thought of that before.

Zepar raised his glass to Ior and Eiltan.

"I hope you are a scotch man. Your son isn't. He never drinks with me. It's a little rude."

"I'm afraid I must be rude too. Scotch is not something the Fae drink. We have our own preferred drinks."

"Maybe we can import Fae liquor to Hell once we seal our alliance."

Ior just grinned.

"Of course. Fae have the best liquor and wine. We'd be happy to share it with Hell. If I had known you wanted to try it, I would have brought some with me. Eiltan told me you preferred to drink scotch at these meetings."

"Yes, I do," Zepar said, knocking back his entire drink.

The potion was almost instantaneous. Zepar's pupils dilated, and he shook his head.

"Something is wrong," he said.

"Are you okay?" Eiltan said.

He got up to check on Zepar. Everything was going according to plan. Until it didn't. Eiltan had barely crossed the coffee table when Zepar opened a portal and disappeared.

We lost him. We failed.

SKÖLL

That big, metal car was quite a thing. Serafina decided she wanted to teach us to drive, and I saw totally different sides of Roman and Amduscias. Roman drove, gripping the wheel, and it hardly felt like the car was moving at all. Amduscias rolled the windows down and drove so fast, I swore we were going to drive straight into a tree and die.

I would have taken Roman for the madman and Amduscias for the granny driver. That's what Serafina kept calling Roman. She kept laughing and telling him he drove like Sophia Petrillo. I had no idea who that was, but she promised to show us when we got home.

Thankfully, she drove us home. If Roman drove, we might never get there, and if Amduscias drove, he might drive us straight through the house. She coasted the car into the driveway and turned it off. Alozan was waiting to fuss over us. She wanted to know what we wanted for lunch.

Serafina gave her this grin that melted my heart.

"I thought I'd show the guys Lebanese food. Can you get that down here?"

"Of course. Akasha's Palace is a personal favorite. The Baba Ganoush there is divine. Don't order out too much. You'll hurt Brinok's feelings if he thinks you don't like his cooking."

I moaned just thinking about Brinok's cooking. The man could roast a leg of venison better than anyone I knew. And those cheeseburgers! I could eat those again.

Amduscias snapped to attention.

"Tell Brinok to cook us a modern feast tonight. I'm still learning all the modern-day foods. I've eaten in several countries before, but something tells me things have changed."

Alozan nodded and disappeared. Serafina wrapped her arms around his waist.

"We should invite Charley and the witches to dinner."

I missed Charley. She met a witch named October almost our first day here and had left to join her coven's compound. None of us had forgotten it was because of Charley that Roman and Serafina were free of Rathmore's spell. I thought we should invite her too. I wanted to see that witch again.

Roman started bouncing. Have you ever seen an enormous Vampire get so excited they can't sit still? That was Roman ever since we got out of Scorchwood. It was nice to see him excited again, but his actions had never matched his angelic face.

"Can we invite Charley? I miss her."

Amduscias gave Roman a gentle smile.

"Of course. Her number should be on my phone. Ah.

Here it is. Why don't all of you go to my bedroom and get settled? I'll invite her."

I didn't care how old I was. I didn't care if it was beneath an Alpha. I didn't care if I looked like Roman. I scooped Serafina up and went running to the bedroom with her. Roman chased after us screaming about his prey drive. I ran up the massive staircase to Amduscias's room. We fell on the bed in a heap of bodies.

"What's the plan, killer?"

"I'm worried about Fergus. He should be meeting with Zepar right about now. Let's order takeout, and I'll show you one of my favorite television shows. It's not super modern, but *The Golden Girls* is a classic. I always put it on when I need cheering up."

I nuzzled her neck.

"Then, we will eat and hold you until Fergus gets back."

"Is Lebanese okay?"

"If it's anything like those Chinese leftovers, it'll be perfect," I said.

"It tastes different, but it's still good."

She whipped out her phone and started fiddling with it. I couldn't decide if it was a miracle or some sort of abomination you could just press a button on your phone and food would show up at your door. I wasn't even used to having a personal chef. Before I got arrested, if I wanted to eat, I had to go into the woods and hunt for it. Who hunted for this Lebanese food we would eat?

Amduscias joined us shortly after. He snuggled into Roman, and we all let out a contented sigh.

"Charley said she'd be happy to come over for dinner. She's heard a little about what's going on in Scorchwood, but she wants the full story. She said if Warden Skinner was behind everything, she'd like a go at her in Bael's dungeon too."

"Fergus should be back now. If that witch potion worked like Eiltan's friends said it would, Zepar should be down here," Serafina said.

She sounded worried. There wasn't a way for Zepar to kill Fergus, but I was wondering if there were wards that could trap him like there had been in Scorchwood. Maybe she was worried about her father and grandfather a little?

She just had them thrust into her life, and they had a long way to go before she trusted them, but I saw the way they looked at her. They desperately wanted her forgiveness and acceptance. Fuck, Ior was changing Fae laws just to let her live.

"There's a time difference, Serafina. It might be noon here, but it's not on Earth. Depending on where they are, the sun might not be up yet."

She tore herself out of our arms and started pacing.

"This is driving me crazy. It feels like I should be doing something. Skinner is in the dungeon, and Zepar is out there somewhere. I'm sitting here ordering takeout and talking about my favorite television shows."

We never fought over her before, and that wasn't natural for my wolf. He should have ripped out all of their throats by now, but then we would have lost her. We wrestled a little now. We were still lying in bed, and we all wanted to hold her. I usually loved sleeping in that vast, plush bed, but now I was trying to get around Roman to get out of it.

I snarled at Roman when he smashed my cock in his haste to get out of bed. Roman hissed at Amduscias when he took his elbow to his eye. We all stopped when we heard Serafina laughing.

"Gel memory foam is not the best platform for a

wrestling match. Sorry, I'm being stupid. I know Fergus can handle it, and I know why I can't be there myself."

There was a soft knock on the door. It must be our food. Don't ask me how they managed to get it to us so fast. Serafina made a move towards the door, and something happened that I never wanted to witness again.

A portal opened in Amduscias's bedroom. It was a demon portal instead of a Fae one. The only reason I knew the difference was because I had seen both, and they were distinct colors.

Two arms reached out and yanked her through. I only knew one demon that would portal her somewhere without talking to Amduscias first or even asking her permission. He could have taken her anywhere.

My wolf roared. I couldn't get to her. Amduscias could open a portal if we knew where he took her. That left one of us.

Fergus better get to her, or I would find a way to kill that dragon.

SERAFINA

I swear, this was the third fucking time someone had kidnapped me, and I was starting to feel like I was in a Liam Neeson movie. No sexy Irishman was coming to save me and bust heads, though. This was all on me. As soon as I felt the arms around my waist, I started fighting, but I was still pulled through the portal.

I only knew three people who would try this shit. Warden Skinner was currently being tortured, I beat the shit out of my father last time, and I hoped he learned his lesson, so that left Zepar. I was starting to doubt any skills I thought I might have developed if I managed to get kidnapped by a demon who should have been roofied.

He was pretty fucked up. He let go of me as soon as we got through the portal. He was supporting himself on a desk, and if this were a cartoon, there would have been drunk birds flying around his head. He looked like he was ready to pass out. He pointed to the ceiling. I saw the same ward from Rathmore's lab.

"I had a plan to bring your father here and ransom the king if it got to where I thought I didn't need the Fae as allies. You'll do in a pinch. I'm sure Ior doesn't want it out that his own son sired a halfling bastard. If he doesn't give me my army, I'll make sure every single realm knows about it."

Okay, first of all, I hadn't let anyone talk to me like that since I accidentally burned the convent down. He warded the room against my Fae powers, but I didn't just rely on those. Fergus told me there would be times it wasn't appropriate to bring out my fire, and I'd have to rely on my fists and wits. That time was now.

I couldn't burn Zepar, but my fire would have been useless against him anyway. He was already drugged. I just needed to help him go to sleep and find a phone. He was already halfway there. I'd been in enough torture dungeons in Hell to recognize where I was. Zepar said he had two estates, but I had a feeling that was a lie. If he would hold a Fae prince hostage, he wouldn't do it in real estate in his name.

I'd murdered men like Zepar. This was probably a house owned by a shell corporation that couldn't be traced back to him. I had no idea where I was, but Zepar just grabbed me, and my phone was still in my back pocket. I just needed to knock a demon out. Easy, right?

Zepar knew I had an edge because he was drugged. I saw a red cloud swirling around him. I'd seen Amduscias break out his demonic form, and that red cloud differed from the one for demon portals. I also saw what that red cloud did to the guards back at Scorchwood.

"Yo, Zepar, I'm really happy for you, and I'm going to let

you finish, but Amduscias had the best demonic reveal of all time."

"Children, I swear," Zepar growled.

His red cloud didn't take as long as Amduscias's did. When it was over, I was just looking at Zepar in a suit of armor. All of this was happening because of him, and yes, I was a bitter bitch about it. I laughed in his face.

"That's it? That's your big, bad demonic form? Amduscias got a unicorn. I could kick your ass even with all that metal on."

"You must have a death wish, halfling bastard. I'm a Duke of Hell. Your own father hates you so much, he experimented on you. I can't kill you because you can get me what I want, but that doesn't mean I can't punish this insolence."

Man, when demon egos raged, they went totally out of control. And I could work with that. He was much older than I was and probably trained in more styles of fighting than I was. I needed him careless to beat him.

"You might get a blow in, but I will brag all over Hell that a halfling beat your ass in a fistfight."

Zepar roared and shoved a chair out of the way. He was still drunker than Cooter Brown and almost fell over. When he faced me, he tried to do it like a boxer. Okay, maybe he wasn't trained in more fighting styles than I was. Perhaps he relied on his legions to do all his fighting. He might be an excellent boxer, but I had been taking Krav Maga classes all over the country since college.

His first punch was aimed at my face. It was sloppy. He was just swinging and hoping to hit me hard enough to do damage. I couldn't punch him in the stomach because he had a full metal breastplate on, but I did use his momentum to shove him to the floor.

I had to remember not to kill him. If I killed him, we lost

the cure for the Fae. I was just so pissed, I saw red. I wanted to rip his head off with my bare hands. I wanted to find something sharp and shove it so far into his ear that his brains came out the other end.

I didn't hesitate. I pounced on his back and put him in a chokehold. He bucked and fought, but I held on like an enraged howler monkey. Zepar was the one howling. I think he put some curse on my first-born child, but I didn't let go. I kept squeezing until he finally shut the fuck up.

That was when I felt it. I wasn't alone anymore. Fergus was with me. He found me like he always did.

"Let go, my Ena. You'll kill him if you keep squeezing. The fate of the Fae lies in your hands right now. Do you want your revenge on Zepar, or can you wait until we have a remedy?"

I let go of Zepar and shrieked. Fergus never asked me not to kill someone before, and I hated that the fate of an entire race was in this fucker's blood. Because I really wanted to spill it right now. I couldn't. I had to wait.

"How do I keep him asleep long enough to get him to Hell? I don't have any idea where I am."

"Hang tight, my Ena. You're in Alaska, and your father is on his way. I've contacted him, and he's coming now with demon warded handcuffs. Zepar will go to Hell just like we wanted. I didn't intend to fail and have you hurt in the process."

"He was too fucked up to lay a finger on me."

"He had to lay a finger on you to get you here. I'm going to have to find a creative way to kill him."

"I think we will have to get in line, Fergus."

Fergus didn't have time to respond because my father and grandfather came charging through. I had no idea I needed this until it happened, but neither of them went straight to Zepar to get handcuffs on him that would neutralize his power.

They came straight to me to check on me and pull me into an enormous hug. I hadn't realized I needed that from either of them until I was smashed into a group hug.

So, I decided I definitely would not kill my father. I would try to get to know him better.

Amduscias

I should have called Bael and let him know the plan had gone ass up, but I was too worried about Serafina. She could be anywhere. Alozan heard the ruckus and had come to see what we were all yelling about. She tried to show us how to track her phone if she had it. Serafina *always* had her phone nearby. It was usually in her pocket unless she was sleeping.

Alozan was trying to explain some nonsense about Wi-Fi and signals because her phone kept saying it wasn't online, and her last location was my house. What good were these damned things, anyway? And where the fuck was Fergus?

I was fiddling with that damned phone while Skoll and Roman reached through their bonds.

"She's north in an undiscovered land. She's so mad right now, I can't reach her through our bond," Skoll said.

"She's in a total rage," Roman said. "The king wants to

spare her life because she's his granddaughter, but if she murders Zepar and loses that cure, he may change his mind."

Serafina was strong, and I didn't doubt she could handle herself. Zepar had always been weak for any demon, much less a Duke of Hell. He had his rank and legions because he was fire born, and that was it. If Dukedoms were given out based on deeds and power, Zepar would never be considered. But he was fire born, and we were tough to kill. Serafina's deadliest weapon was useless against us.

I knew Zepar. He was throwing a tantrum, and that made him dangerous. He realized Eiltan betrayed him, and Hell might be onto him. I knew precisely why he grabbed Serafina. Blackmail. But since Eiltan wasn't there to take the brunt of his rage, Serafina would do since she was his daughter.

I was getting so frustrated.

"If you can reach her, can either of you talk to Fergus?" I asked.

Roman ran his fingers through his hair.

"Don't you think if I were an expert at contacting an ancient Fae spirit, I would have done it by now? It's still like someone jumping out and yelling *boo* when he just starts talking to me in my head."

It was like someone jumped out and yelled *boo* when my cell phone started ringing. I jumped about fifty feet and nearly flung it against the wall. Luckily, it never left my hand. I checked the caller ID desperately hoping to see Serafina's face, but it was Bael.

"You should have called and told me Zepar took your mate," Bael chided.

"Did Alozan tell you?"

Bael just laughed.

"No, she's in my dungeon with Zepar and her family. I might not even need my toys to torture him. He's always been prideful. Taunting him with the fact that a halfling half his size incapacitated him should do worse than my pliers could."

"Bael, we can talk about what an asshole Zepar is later. I just watched Serafina disappear into a portal. I think we all need to see her and make sure she's okay."

"Well, didn't I just fucking invite you? Someone needs to calm her down. Most all the pain in her life is because of Zepar, and she wants him dead five minutes ago."

"I'm hanging up and coming over."

"None of you can kill him for taking her. I'm warning you, Amduscias. Tell the wolf and the Vampire they can't get their revenge just yet. We need to know who he recruited, and we still need his blood. I'm getting that now."

I hung up the phone and faced my friends.

"She's safe at Bael's dungeon, and Zepar is still alive. We need him alive for now, so no killing just yet."

"Yeah, but who gets to kill him when the time comes? He hurt Serafina, and she's our mate. Hell wants him dead, and so do the Fae. Do we draw straws?"

I already knew how that would go down, but it was better explained in detail later.

"It will be done publicly and quite graphically. Let's get to our mate now."

I opened a portal to Bael's dungeon. I didn't know what kind of mood she would be in, but I could only guess. I just knew I wanted to take her in my arms and hold her until she was happy again.

ROMAN

We all went charging through the portal. I was screaming Serafina's name and looking around for her wildly. She was standing in the corner, surrounded by her family and the faint outline of a golden man. I guess she had started the process of making Fergus real. She saw me looking for her and went running at me. She flung herself in my arms, and I squeezed her as hard as I could.

After I'd gotten my hugs, she turned to Skoll and Amduscias. I finally took in the surrounding scene. I smelled blood. I always smelled blood down here. Sometimes it was faint, but with Warden Skinner down here, it was a lot stronger. I could see where it was coming from now.

They strung Zepar up by his heels with a tube in his carotid draining blood into bags. That looked uncomfortable, but that was still too good for him. He kidnapped my

Serafina, and he deserved to die. I wanted to rip his throat out.

Zepar was still totally out. I slung my arm around her shoulder.

"What did you do to him?" I asked proudly.

"Jumped on his back and choked him. That's not all me. They injected him with something so he stays out."

"I recognized the ingredients in the potion the witches gave him. They interact in a way that he will be sleeping for hours," a voice said.

I turned around, and Charley was standing there.

"Charley!" I cried. I bounded over to her and pulled her into a huge hug. "You just left us for your witch friends. I miss you."

Charley laughed as I spun her around.

"I missed you too, Roman. I came because I know a spell to get into Zepar's mind."

Bael puffed up his chest.

"And we don't punish witches for that down here unless they use it for mischief. Tell me more, Charley. Is it going to hurt him?"

"I can make it hurt."

"Excellent."

Ior looked a little ill.

"Is that enough blood to cure the Fae?"

Doctor Bogthon was there supervising. He might have been the one to set up the device draining all the blood from Zepar. It just looked so complicated. I'd stick to biting and my fangs, though hanging someone upside down could be useful. I'd have to experiment with that if I needed to eat someone creatively. It would be like those straw things Serafina showed everyone when they had milkshakes.

"Oh, I could have made a cure just by pricking his finger

and getting a drop. But since it was his blood that caused this entire mess, we decided to make the cure by ridding him of most of it," Doctor Bogthon said.

"What is that much of his blood going to do to the Fae?" Eiltan asked.

"How did you manage to lose him?" Skoll growled. "He took Serafina."

I wanted to know that too. How hard was it to keep track of one demon? I mean, it seems like they found him pretty quickly again. Why couldn't they find him before he touched my mate?

"He felt the drug kick in and portalled away before I could get to him. It was so fast. I kept the distance between us short so that wouldn't happen. Understand, they had tested this potion on other supernaturals, but never a demon before. Zepar felt it kick in and portalled away. Don't ask me why he thought to kidnap my daughter while he was still drugged. Many men will make the folly of underestimating her."

"Like you did?" Amduscias sniffed.

"Yes, even me."

Just then, one of Bael's servants burst into the door with four demons in battle armor. Bael snapped to attention.

"You're one of Zepar's legion. I see the crests of Agares, Gusion, and Saleos. What is it you want?"

"A way out," a demon said. "Gusion is asking us to attack the kings to free Zepar. Agares has sent his soldiers that agreed to fight to attack the gates of Hell to let outsiders in to join the fight. Gusion is organizing everything."

"You. You're Zepar's men. Did you know about his plot to overthrow Hell?"

"None of us knew, sir. We've all settled into our lives and started families. We haven't been called on to fight in so long, we didn't think we would be. Suddenly, we've got Dukes barking orders at us that there is going to be a regime change. We're supposed to break Zepar out of Bael's dungeon and help outsiders overthrow the seven kings.

"Several soldiers decided to do their duty and are forming ranks, but there are also those of us that are happy with the way things are. I can speak for several of us in Zepar's legion that we've never liked him and don't want to see him as king of Hell. The same goes for the other men here. They don't want to see their commander as king either."

Bael slammed his fist on a metal slab in the dungeon and started swearing.

"Looks like we need that army after all. I will rally the kings. Amduscias, I'm counting on you to get the Dukes in order. Solron, stay behind and guard our prisoners. I'll get you some more demons. I want the four of you where I can see you. I'm not sure if this is part of the plot to free Zepar. A Trojan Horse, if you will."

A demon bowed his head like he understood.

"Agares has thirty-one legions. He sent them all to attack the gates of Hell. Ten have defected and are just awaiting orders. They will defend the gates if needed."

Eiltan snapped to attention. He may have fucked everything up from the start, but maybe he wasn't totally worthless. I mean, he had to have a little of Serafina in him.

"The Fae should defend the gates from topside. There's no point in letting the people in this little rebellion grow by letting more people into Hell. Zepar is not well liked. Most of the people who joined him were either blackmailed or paid. All we have to do is stop them long enough to tell them Zepar will get what's coming to them, and they aren't getting any of the money promised, and that should thin their numbers."

"Still, those words are best said with an army to back you up, son. Let's get back to the Fae realm and gather men."

Eiltan and Ior disappeared into a portal. Things were chaos in the dungeon. I thought this would be over when we captured Zepar. All these demons trying to rally and still carry out his plan with him caught reminded me of someone I killed before they arrested me. I kept draining their blood, and their heart should have long stopped, but they kept getting up and trying to fight me, even if they could hardly throw a punch.

I was killing that person instead of just drinking their blood without their permission because he had a foul habit of raping women, and I couldn't abide by that.

Why was it always the evil people who couldn't accept defeat gracefully? Now, we would have to go out and kill more people because these fucking Dukes didn't realize it was over. Even their own legions didn't want to fight for them, and I had a feeling the ones that did were on the battle lines because they were following orders.

I'd fight right alongside these demons, but I hoped I got to kill the right people. We were all killers, but I think we could all agree murder was wrong unless you were killing the right person.

There were several of the right people that needed to die right now.

SERAFINA

All I had to say was that someone had snatched me three times, I'd been experimented on and insulted, and I knocked out a drugged-up Duke of Hell by myself. I didn't care who they were. If someone tried to sideline me for this fight, they would not like my reaction.

I thought this was finally over as I watched Zepar being strung up by his feet. I talked to Fergus, and he agreed it was finally time. I couldn't celebrate that I could finally wish Fergus real, and I could see a faint outline of the man I saw in my dreams when I was awake because Zepar was still shitting in my cornflakes.

I hadn't spent all that much time around him, but I was shocked he'd managed to find friends willing to rescue his ass. If I was a corrupt demon working with Zepar, and he got caught before he even gathered his army, I'd get someone in Bael's dungeon to kill him before he uttered my name and dragged me down with him, not rescue his uppity ass.

He was a miserable bastard with a raging ego. If I could have killed him when I had my elbow wrapped around his neck, I totally would have. I'm sure Zepar's death would have stopped this little Hell rebellion, but it would have meant the end of the Fae. The fact that he was continually fucking up my life, even before I knew who he was, meant I was joining this fight no matter who didn't want me to.

Amduscias had already portalled us back to his place, and he had a war room in his palace. His servants had it updated and were in there working as soon as they heard what was up. There were television screens up with video chat with all the Dukes of Hell that weren't utter fuckups. They all admitted they never liked Zepar either.

Everything was buzzing and moving a million miles a minute. I wanted to be involved, but it wasn't like I had my own legion I could call on like certain demons in Hell. I didn't even have an army at my disposal like my father. I had fire and piss and vinegar running through my veins with no outlet right now.

The more I heard them talk, I realized how ass-backward this plan was. There were three Dukes and what was left of their legions after several defected trying to rescue Zepar and overthrow Hell. I knew there were seven kings of Hell. On the screens and in this room were at least nineteen Dukes with their own legions willing to quash them. And I knew there were other demons like Solron who were loyal to the kings and would fight. I think I spoke for my mates when I said we were all sitting here ready to cut a bitch too.

"You said the Fae are defending the gates topside?" a Duke said.

"The king and prince left to gather soldiers. They seem

to work quickly, but I've got no idea if they've made it there yet," Amduscias said. "The gates are heavily guarded by demons on both sides. I'm not sure how much time we had before we were tipped off, but I doubt they have fallen just yet."

"What is the plan, Amduscias?"

"Gather your legions. They need to be divided. Some need to be sent to reinforce the king's legions should the gates fall. Zepar has assassins picked for each king. Choose however many you think are needed to defend your estate. Don't think Zepar doesn't intend to kill us to secure his reign. The rest of our legions are required in order to protect the gate.

"Agares, Gusion, and Saleos will be holed up in their estates, letting their legions do their dirty work. They never liked getting their hands dirty, and we already know that's how they've fought every battle when their legions have been called upon.

"They will have reinforcements and a legion at home to defend them. We already know several of their legions have defected. We can use that. We need to split up and approach each estate. Give their legions the option to lay down arms. If those men were right, they knew nothing of this plot, and I have no desire to kill them because they were following orders.

"We need to step up. Give them a place in one of our legions or offer them an out. They can become a civilian if they lay down their arms and let us enter the estate to capture their master. Zepar will be tortured, then publicly executed. His cohorts deserve the same fate. If they can't be captured alive, kill them."

"Saleos will come without a fight. He's a pacifist which is why I've got no idea why he's a part of this. Agares is weak in his demonic form, but his crocodile is no joke. Gusion's baboon is wholly unpleasant if he tries to fight in his demonic form. It would be best to try to take him before he whips that out."

"Fergus, can you get inside him now that I've started to wish you real? If you fly into his mouth, we can threaten him and stop him from shifting. His blood isn't some magical cure. We can still kill him."

"I'm between the veil now, my Ena. I'm not a spirit, but I'm not real just yet. I'm having issues calling on my powers to shift. All of this is forbidden, so I don't know what my powers will be when you wish me real. Your dragon might be gone."

"But you'll be real, and I'll be able to touch you. I wish you real, Fergus. Be real for me."

That was the second time I wished it. The first time I did, I felt this brief surge go through me and could faintly see Fergus. The swell was more forceful this time, and Fergus got even more substantial. It was almost like I could reach out and touch his beautiful face. I tried, and my hand passed straight through.

I had forgotten we had an audience of all the Dukes of Hell that weren't complete tools watching us until I heard one of them address me.

"We could use all the opinions we can get on this, Amduscias. If your halfling princess can make the Fae spirit come to life now, it's probably the time for it."

I scowled at the demon on the screen. Yes, I wanted Fergus real as soon as I could, and yes, he could help. It just felt like when Fergus finally became real, and I could touch him outside of my dreams, it should be a special, private moment. Not in a war room full of demons that just wanted his opinion. I was shocked when I heard Fergus speak out loud because I certainly couldn't touch him.

"Ask me what you will, but the moment my Ena wishes me real will be a private moment between us. I can still protect her like this."

The one demon who seemed to be itching for me to rush something special squinted at the screen like he was trying to make out Fergus's hazy form.

"The Fae do this sort of thing all the time, but no one has ever tried to overthrow the monarchy in all of Hell's history. What kind of advice can you give us, so this ends with as little lives lost as possible?"

"Zepar is the instigator. All of this is happening because of him. We have what we need from him to cure the Fae. I know Hell wants to torture him so he suffers for his crimes, but the quickest way to stop a rebellion is to execute the usurper publicly and swiftly. The Fae would have done it as soon as they made sure they had his blood, so they didn't have a second war with the people he fucked over."

Every single demon on the screen looked totally scandalized by that, but it made sense. I was sure Zepar had promised those Dukes something if they helped him, but with Zepar dead, what were they other than insurgents with no leader and no backup?

"Only a king of Hell can order the execution of someone of Zepar's rank," someone said.

Amduscias was the only one who could see any sense in all of this, and that was why I loved him. None of the other Dukes would harm a hair on Zepar's head without permission, so Amduscias just called Bael and got it, so there was no division among Hell royalty. Bael really wanted to torture him, but even he could see the logic behind a swift execution.

Amduscias hung up the phone and addressed the other Dukes.

"Bael said to kill him in the town square but to make it memorable so no one gets any ideas in the future. He also said while we are doing that, move on to the original plan. Send your legions to defend the gates and capture the other Dukes. Bael has one edict. Serafina gets to choose Zepar's method of execution. He likes her style, and Zepar did a lot of nasty things to her. He feels bad he didn't get her a gift when she arrived. This is your housewarming gift, Serafina. Choose wisely."

Well, fuck. If that wasn't the best present I'd ever gotten in my entire life, I'd be a horse's ass. I needed to make it unique. All of Hell was watching, and I hadn't forgotten the things he said to me before I knocked him out.

This would be the best death I'd ever plotted. I also needed to come up with it quickly.

FERGUS

Being between the veil was no joke. I wasn't a spirit anymore. I couldn't reach out to the other guardians if I wanted to. I hadn't since I felt Serafina and having her was more important than talking to spirits, but it was strange. I couldn't travel between realms with just a thought anymore, but I also couldn't touch her yet, and that was killing me.

I didn't know much about guardians who became real before because they were usually hunted and killed. Everyone, guardian and Fae, thought it was so taboo, it was never discussed. I didn't know what powers I would have once I was alive again. I could feel my Fae magic, but the only thing I could access right now was my fire.

I don't think Bael realized the gift he had given Serafina, letting her choose how Zepar would die. It would give her closure, and it would warm that little bit of darkness that resided in her. It needed to be unique. It couldn't be a repeat of something we had done before. This had to be an individual, one of a kind execution.

She chewed her bottom lip.

"If my fire won't kill him, how does one kill a Duke of Hell?"

Good question. Fire ran through her veins. It would seem off to kill Zepar without fire. It was how we killed everyone who came across our radar as deserving it. It was the only method she ever used to kill. I knew this meant a lot to her, and she wanted to impress people with this. Hell and the Fae realm would want to know Zepar died spectacularly for what he did.

Amduscias was just grinning like a total fool.

"Fire won't burn him, but hot things still bother us. You could heat up something and use it to kill him."

"Could I boil him alive? Like, stick him in a huge vat of oil and boil the flesh from his bones?"

We were in the middle of a massive pile of shit, and Amduscias decided to flirt. He would always bat his long lashes when he wanted to tease, and he was fluttering them all over the place right now.

"You certainly know the right words to turn a demon on. Yes, that would kill Zepar."

I didn't know Charley that well, but she'd come in extremely helpful when we were in Scorchwood. I hadn't forgotten my Ena would still be under Rathmore's spell if it wasn't for her. I thought she felt like an extra wheel in Amduscias's palace with everyone being in a relationship here, and she left to join a coven as soon as she met a witch. I was glad she was here now.

"Ooh, can I make a suggestion if you're boiling him in oil? There's a forbidden potion my father taught me. It's like breaking out in syphilis sores all over your body."

Serafina pulled Charley into a hug and kissed her on the cheek.

"Have I mentioned how much I love you? Is there anything else we can give him besides syphilis before I boil him alive?"

Charley was this tiny, cherubic looking witch, and I didn't really think she deserved a life sentence in Scorchwood for a mistake made in grief, but she clearly had a wicked side. I had a feeling if she started coming over more, she and Serafina would be quite excellent friends.

"Oh, I know all kinds of forbidden potions and curses. My father learned them from the witches and warlocks he had to arrest. He taught them to me just in case. I've got a spell from a warlock who was mad a woman turned him down that will make all his body hair fall out, and I've got another one from a witch that caught her husband in bed with another woman that will turn his cock the size of a peanut."

I could see the wheels in Serafina's head turning. Typically, when we killed someone, it was quick, and we didn't play with our food. It wasn't just that she wanted to impress people with this. Zepar indirectly caused every bad thing in her life by cursing the Fae women. The only good I could see in Zepar was that if he hadn't, Eiltan wouldn't have been spending so much time on Earth to sire Serafina.

Still, if the situation back in the Fae realm hadn't been so dire, Eiltan wouldn't have been gone so long. He might have come back before her mother realized she was having a strange pregnancy and fled to a convent. Serafina would have had a much different upbringing.

For that alone, I would have killed Zepar horribly. But he didn't just hurt my Ena. He hurt innocent Fae women, and for that, he deserved to be humiliated before he died. I hoped everyone there had cameras out, and photos of Zepar with no eyebrows and his microcock went viral in every single realm he hurt people in.

"Can I bite him too?" Roman asked. "He deserves a big, painful Vampire bite for hurting my mate."

Skoll wasn't one to be left out either.

"After you make his cock small, can my wolf rip it off? My wolf needs him to feel pain for hurting you."

We all wanted a go at Zepar for what he did to her, but I would be content with Serafina getting her revenge. Maybe it would help her put everything behind her, and we could find peace here in Hell.

"What about you, Amduscias? Do you want to hurt him too?"

There were those eyelashes again. Only Amduscias would get off on planning an execution.

"I will be watching and enjoying the show, Serafina. I plan on using the camera on that cell phone to record the whole thing, and I'm going to post it all over those social media sites you were showing me. Zepar, with a tiny cock and syphilis, will get a ton of laughs down here, and I think everyone would agree boiling him alive is a brilliant way to die. I also plan to have my wicked way with you after I watch you do all that."

Amduscias had referred to me as a horny dragon more than once, but at least I wasn't planning to get laid while there was an active threat going on in Hell. Killing Zepar would not end it right away.

Serafina just pulled him into a kiss.

"We have to stop the other Dukes and all the people trying to break into Hell first."

AMDUSCIAS

Zepar wasn't the first Duke of Hell to be executed. There was one before him who never managed to be written about and never got his own legions. He was a young fire born Bael never liked. Zagan liked a challenge and took him under his wing. This particular Duke was raping and murdering lesser demons. The kings of Hell wouldn't stand for rape, much less murder. He was beheaded swiftly in the town square after being tortured for a few decades.

I was glad Bael decided to make an example of Zepar. Letting Serafina pick the method was perfect because she could be just as twisted as a demon. She didn't disappoint when she told me what she had planned. We just needed to get Zepar out of Bael's dungeon and into the town square. Last I checked, he was still hanging upside down getting drained of blood.

I commanded twenty-nine legions. I left four to guard

my estate, one to defend each king, three for each Duke, two to stand guard while we were executing Zepar, and the rest were sent to the gates of Hell.

I was standing in the town square on the stage we had theatre performances on. A sizeable crowd was gathering of all residents of Hell. Two of my best commanders led Zepar out in warded chains. He was still pretty groggy, but immediately perked up when he realized where he was.

"You can't do this to me. Don't you know who I am?" he yelled.

Serafina practically skipped onto the stage, and I don't think I'd ever been more turned on in my life when she started taunting him. She got right up in his face, and I had no idea he said some things to her. Maybe I did want to hurt him instead of watching.

"How does it feel that a halfling bastard is carrying out your execution? I cooked up something special just for you."

Zepar just sneered at her.

"I will die a Duke. Your own family will demand Bael turn you over so they can kill you."

"I neglected to mention I already met my father and grandfather when you kidnapped me. They have no intention of killing me, and Hell got a Fae army, it's just stopping yours."

Zepar tried to lunge at her. They wrapped him in demon warded chains. I'm not sure what he was expecting to do other than head butting her. She wasn't having any of that. Serafina just stepped back and punched him right in the face. I could hear his nose break from where I was standing.

Two of the biggest demons I'd ever seen dragged him away from her and tied him to a big metal post. Zepar might be immune to her fire, but his clothing wasn't. She wanted him naked and humiliated before he died. He deserved it too. She flicked her wrist, and his clothes turned to ash.

I was glad someone called Charley for this. She'd been accommodating in Scorchwood with her knowledge of forbidden spells, but she was also a twisted fuck when she was sober, and sometimes, she was the only one who could make Roman laugh when he was in a mood.

Only Charley would have suggested giving a Duke of Hell syphilis and a tiny cock before they executed him, and only Serafina would have heard that idea and decided to break it out during a public execution. When Hell decided someone needed to die, sure, we tortured them until they were nearly dead, but that was done in private. When the time came for that person to die, sometimes it was private, and sometimes it was public. Even when it was public, it was done quickly with no pomp and circumstance.

Zepar deserved everything that was coming to him. He earned the humiliation, and he deserved it from someone he looked down on. He hurt people in three realms for this plot. He said some horrible things to someone I loved.

Charley joined Serafina on the platform and handed her two vials. Little Charley walked over to Zepar and punched him in the stomach. What the fuck had he done to her? As far as I knew, they had never met. I guess everyone hated Zepar. Charley spat in his face too.

"That's for what you did to October."

I think only those of us on the podium heard her, but I was dying to know what Zepar did to Charley's witch friend to get that reaction. Zepar looked down on anyone that wasn't a demon. I knew he carelessly slept his way through several of the female demons, and most of them knew not to go anywhere near him. I loved gossip, and I'd have to get it from Charley later. It was time to watch Zepar pay for his crimes.

Charley must have talked to Serafina about what happened with October because she knew something I didn't. Serafina pranced over to Zepar, dangling one of the vials.

"I heard you spread a rash to two in the covens down here because you couldn't keep it in your pants. I heard you knew you had it and kept sleeping around anyway. What do you say, folks? Should we give him magical syphilis?"

"You wouldn't dare! I'm a Duke."

The crowd disagreed. They all wanted to see him with syphilis. I think some women in the crowd were cheering extra hard for it. It was almost instantaneous. Serafina sprinkled the potion on his head, and he immediately started breaking out in sores all over his body.

Just then, the entire crowd hit the ground as a loud crack filled the air. People started yelling about a gun. Who brought a firearm to Hell? With all the demonic powers going on, we didn't need guns to subdue or kill someone.

Unless something had seriously changed while I was in jail, the only reason someone would have a gun at Zepar's execution would be to rescue him.

Either the gates were breached, or he had more supporters than we knew.

SERAFINA

I wasn't stupid. When someone opened fire, you hit the floor. But whoever took that shot wasn't shooting up the crowd. It was one shot, then total silence. No one was screaming in pain like they were hit. We knew the gates of Hell were under attack, and the other Dukes were trying to rescue Zepar. This made little sense.

"Who is hit?" a giant demon yelled.

No one replied, and no one screamed that someone next to them was dead. So, what the fuck was going on?

"Zepar is dead!" someone yelled.

I looked up, and sure enough, someone got Zepar right between the eyes. Someone had straight-up ruined my first public execution that I put a lot of thought into planning. I didn't have time to pout and think about who just ruined my revenge. There was someone out there with a gun. We didn't know if they killed Zepar for one of the other Dukes in on this plot, or they just hated him and didn't want to wait for me to finish. Were the gates breached?

Sweet Roman didn't care about guns. Neither did Skoll. All they cared about was that someone took a shot at Zepar while I was standing next to him. Roman took off using his Vampire speed. Skoll's clothes shredded to bits as he shifted and bounded after him. Red started swirling around Amduscias, and I guess he was breaking his unicorn out.

Fergus was hovering right next to me.

"Make your final wish, my Ena. I know we both wanted it to be special, but the gates of Hell might be breached, and that gunman might not be alone. We need every available fighter."

I sighed. I knew he was right. I was expecting this moment to happen over candlelight when I was ass naked, then we would all get kinky, but Zepar had to ruin that too. You know what? I was glad he was dead, even if it wasn't the idea I came up with. I couldn't even make a big, special speech with my last wish because there could be snipers all over the place.

"Fergus, I wish you real."

God damn, that was so hollow. After everything we had been through together, it came down to this fucking moment on the podium and me with my face practically a stone.

I felt someone pull me to my feet. I was looking at Fergus in the flesh. He was the same beautiful man from my dreams with golden hair and bright eyes. He was wearing strange armor that must have been the style with the Fae when he died. He still had his weapons. There was a bow and satchel of arrows strapped to his back and a sword at his belt.

Fergus stood in front of me and whipped an arrow out.

He aimed into the crowd who had all either hit the floor or fled. Amduscias came back to the platform. He was still a man, and the swirling red cloud was gone.

"Roman found the assassin. It's a shifter."

Roman flashed back up to the stage, holding a man by the neck, and Skoll wasn't far behind him. Roman started waving the shifter in the air. He was so proud he caught him, but the man's neck was flopping at an odd angle.

"I think you broke him, Roman."

Roman turned him around and looked at him. He dropped him on the floor and nudged him with his foot. Roman looked totally devastated.

"Aw, I didn't mean to kill him. He just put up a fight."

Amduscias pulled him into a hug.

"It's okay, Roman. We would have killed him anyway. People! The gunman is dead! Does anyone know this shifter?"

No one knew him. He must have been snuck into Hell. Amduscias grabbed us all.

"We need to get back to my war room. We don't know if they have breached the gates, and we need to find out who this shifter was working for. I need to talk to the other Dukes."

Amduscias opened a portal, but before we could step through, Fergus grabbed me and kissed me so profoundly, my knees turned to jelly.

"More on that later," he said, pulling me through the portal.

AMDUSCIAS

What the actual fuck is going on in Hell? I spend a few hundred years in jail and come back to war. Shifters were getting into Hell and taking potshots at Dukes to ruin well-planned executions. I already knew Zepar was killed by another Duke who had turned against us. If I had to put money on who would betray him, it would be Gusion. Gusion would have hired a shifter to do it too.

I needed to regroup. I opened a portal back to my war room. Roman was still apologizing for killing the shifter before we could question him, Skoll was totally naked, and Fergus was now real looking like a character out of one of the movies Serafina showed us with small men with hairy feet. It was chaos.

"What is going on with the gates?" I demanded.

Barbatos just gave me this steely look. If I could trust any Duke in Hell, it would be him.

"The rebellion at the gate is over. They all took one look at the legions heading towards them and were willing to stop long enough to listen. They've turned on their commanders and have been offered the chance to join another legion or become a civilian after this fight. They've all joined the Fae topside to stop people from breaking in."

"A little late for that," Valefar said. "That shifter that killed Zepar wasn't a resident here. None of the shifters who live here would use a gun to kill. Your Vampire friend broke it before we could torture it for information."

Skoll let out a little growl. I liked Valefar, but he did have an unpleasant habit of looking down on anyone who wasn't a demon. Serafina wasn't having any of that either. She came to stand next to me and gave Valefar some epic stink eye.

"My mate is a shifter. I'd be cautious about how you talk about them."

"Can your mate put some clothes on?" Aym asked.

Serafina wagged her finger at the screen.

"Eyes above the waist, buddy. He may have to shift again. This isn't over just because the gates are safe. Last time I checked, you've still got three Dukes out there, and one may have snuck a shifter down here to kill Zepar. They may have snuck assassins down here for all of you."

Barbatos scratched his goatee. If I could plan all of this with him instead of all the other Dukes, I could probably get more done. We had always been copacetic, and I didn't even visit him when I got back to say hello.

"Saleos hates fighting, but he's still a soldier. He would have planned for all scenarios, including Zepar getting caught. Saleos would be plotting to protect his domicile and not go down with him. Saleos could have snuck an assassin down here so he wouldn't go down with him. I'd also put money on Gusion working behind everyone's back to seize the throne once they had done all the work. He's always pretended to have an affinity with the shifters because his demonic form is a baboon. It's always been to use them."

"Well, if a sniper was waiting for Zepar, then there's an excellent chance there are several waiting outside at at least one of the Duke's houses waiting for a king or Duke to show up," Serafina pointed out.

"Can I go sniper hunting?" Roman said with a little bounce. "I already killed one of them."

Serafina just shrugged. "They aren't immune to fire. Fergus, do you still have fire?"

I watched Fergus shift into a fire dragon again. He was small, so he wouldn't incinerate my entire war room and kill Skoll and Roman, and for that, I was grateful. Like I needed him destroying my shit to prove a point. He instantly shifted back, and now the horny little dragon had a real face to grin at her with.

"Now that I'm not between the veil, I can experiment with my powers. I've kept some of my guardian powers. I can still be your fire dragon."

"That's so sexy," she growled. "Can we go out and kill some bad guys?"

I knew better than to tell her no when she got all murdery. We all had a stake in this fight. It wouldn't do if a random sniper picked off a king of Hell with a spelled bullet. But who was more likely to have snuck snipers down here?

Agares was always more of a follower and a weak Duke. He was also very greedy, but he was very lazy. He wouldn't have wanted to be a king because it was too much work, but he would have wanted money and more soldiers in his legions. If they promised him women, he would do anything for them, that would have just sweetened the pot for him. No, there would be no snipers at his place. I had a feeling the other kings just used him for his resources.

That left Saleos and Gusion. Saleos never fought if he could avoid it. He used to have a healthy respect for a soldier's life. If I had to make a roster of all the Dukes that would have been involved in this, I wouldn't have picked Saleos. He always seemed to have some sort of honor code that he lived by. I was never friendly with him, but before all this, I respected him. There had to be some reason he would have joined this rebellion that I just didn't know.

That left Gusion, who I never liked. I disliked him as much as I had disliked Zepar. Gusion would be the one with the snipers.

"Get ready. All of you send three legions to back up the kings at Agares and Saleos. We need everyone at Gusion's. I'm almost one hundred percent certain Gusion has the snipers and still thinks he can seize the throne."

"I agree," Barbatos said. "But if he breaks out that infernal baboon, your unicorn is dealing with him."

FERGUS

This wasn't how I wanted things to play out. I thought it would end with Zepar's death, and my Ena and I could have a special moment when she wished me real. All the demons I had met so far had this honor code they lived by, even if I didn't agree with the torture thing. I guessed when a demon broke that code, they went way out.

Zepar organized this entire thing, and I put all the blame on him. Still, it was a little poetic that the demon that cursed the Fae and plotted to murder Hell royalty didn't even have enough friends in Hell that wouldn't either dance at his execution or stab him in the back to take his place.

I knew my Ena could handle herself in a fight. She had her fire, and she had taken fight lessons. Snipers were a different story. All it took was one spelled bullet, and any one of us could die. I could be ripped away from Serafina now that I was flesh. I wouldn't get a second chance at being her guardian. I didn't know what happened to the guardians who were wished real before me and were killed by the Fae, but I know they didn't get their old duties back after they died a second time.

I was grateful I could still become pure fire. That was leftover from my guardian days, and I could use it now. I would burn every hiding place a sniper could be if it kept her safe. I might be flesh now, but I would always be her guardian.

I didn't want to jump into a portal to anyone's palace until we had a plan. If there was one thing I learned while I was alive was that portalling into the middle of a battle meant people would die. There was always a telltale sign that a portal was being opened, and the enemy always aimed for it because it meant reinforcements were coming.

Amduscias wasn't stupid, and he knew that. The screens were still up with all the Dukes of Hell that hadn't gone rogue. The rest of the Dukes clearly knew war strategy too. Gusion lived in a different area than Amduscias did. Amduscias lived by the beach, and Gusion lived in a more wooded area. I didn't like it. There were too many places for snipers to hide, and they had chastised Serafina and me against burning the forest down because most of the trees were sentient. No one knew if the trees had joined the fight, and we wouldn't know that until we got there. We also didn't know whose side the trees would be on.

Everyone was discussing points to portal in where they might not notice us until we wanted to be. Unfortunately, those were the perfect places for a sniper to be hiding. We had to bank on the fact that Gusion wouldn't have had as much time to network topside as Zepar did because he wasn't allowed to live there full time. Still, this was war, and you should never underestimate the enemy.

We finally had a place we could agree on. It meant walking on foot, but this is also where I could become of use. Since I could still become pure fire, I could control the size of the flame. I could become a mere ember and scout ahead. I also had permission to burn anyone with a gun as long as I didn't destroy any tree demons.

Serafina pulled me into a passionate kiss after we stepped through the portal and into a forest. She squeezed me so tight, and I had to enjoy it while I could. We had to stop this before she could have a home here, and if it meant dying to defend her, I would. Of course, I wanted to avoid that at all costs.

"You'd better come back to me, Fergus," she warned.

I kissed the tip of her nose. I reached out to her with my mind. Even though we had broken every single rule, and she wished me real, I was still linked to her as her guardian, and we could talk telepathically. I reached out to Roman and Skoll too, because I was now connected to them through her.

"You'd better stay put until I give the all-clear, my Ena. If she dies on your watch, I will hold all of you responsible and end you."

Skoll was still as naked as the day he was born and didn't seem to care who saw, but he was a shifter, and they liked to show off. Roman had that antsy look on his face like he either had to go to the bathroom or kill someone. Amduscias was casually checking out his fingernails.

"We'll keep her safe. You don't have to worry about that," Skoll growled.

Amduscias started with the eyelashes again. That demon could flirt in the middle of the apocalypse.

"How'd you like to ride a unicorn, Serafina? I've got something else you can ride later."

I knew that shriek that came out of her mouth. She was never a girl who was into sparkly stickers with unicorns on them, but a demon unicorn? That was right up her alley. She probably didn't even know she liked black unicorns with red eyes until Amduscias whipped it out and started goring people with his horn. She'd never even ridden a horse before, but getting to ride a big demonic unicorn was like getting the best gift she didn't know she wanted.

I gave Amduscias a curt nod and reduced myself to an ember. We had an unspoken understanding. If she was on his back, she couldn't come running after me if she thought I was in danger. And she would. She'd run into a sniper infested nest if she felt any of us would be hurt.

I hated tricking her like this, but it was better I get hurt than her. Her life was finally starting to look up. She found her mates, and it seemed like she was willing to get to know her family. Plus, I could shrink myself, and she couldn't. I taught her to protect herself, but why risk it?

I flew through the forest as barely a spark. It didn't take long to find the snipers. Everyone was worried about us hurting the tree demons, but it looked like they could take care of themselves. No one knew whose side they were on when we left, and now I could see it wasn't Gusion's.

Two shifters, two Vampires, and three warlocks were trapped in a nest of tree roots. The tree demons were quite beautiful. They looked like androgynous, thin beings with elongated arms and legs and cascading leaves for hair. They had a mean set of teeth, though, and a temper to match.

One of them nearly had a warlock racked with her roots and was dangling his gun in front of him. She sneered at him and practically ripped his shoulders out of the socket.

"Who do you work for?" she yelled. "Why are you in our forest with guns?"

I immediately transformed back into a man. I didn't want to get ensnared in tree roots, but I wasn't sure the proper reverence to show to a tree demon. Who was in charge, anyway? I just pretended I was at Fae court and gave them all a deep bow. I kept my eyes averted until I was addressed and given permission to speak because that was just how things were done back in the Fae realm when you were just a soldier in a court of kings, lords, and ladies.

"Oh, get up, you silly fairy," a tree snarled. "You'd better have a good reason for being in our forest, or I'll truss you up too."

"These men are assassins hired by Gusion. There's a coup going on in Hell, and you probably turned the tide capturing these men. I'm a scouting party, and I'm working with the Duke Amduscias. I was trying to find snipers. We know Zepar had seven assassins picked for each king, but we caught Zepar and planned to execute him. A sniper took out Zepar, so we are pretty sure Gusion intended to betray him and hired his own assassins."

All the trees started laughing, and a tree demon's laugh was a little creepy. It was like sawing wood, if that could be evil. One of the tree demons that wasn't stretching a sniper so hard they might rip a limb off got right in my face. I was tall for a Fae, but he towered over me. His face had fine lines on it like tree bark, and his eyes glowed an eerie shade of green.

"Gusion has always treated this forest like it was his. He tramples through this forest hunting game, and he relieves himself on tree demons like we are nothing. He allowed these men with guns to besmirch our sacred woods. If capturing these men hurts Gusion, then good. We will kill them."

I couldn't imagine what it would be like to be killed by a

tree, but I didn't want to find out. They seemed pretty temperamental about their forest, and I was trespassing. I honestly didn't care who killed the assassins. They were filthy creatures with no honor. But we needed to ask them questions first.

I bowed my head again and didn't make eye contact.

"Of course, you have every right to kill these men for bringing guns into your forest. I know I'm asking a lot, but can Amduscias and a few more people come to your forest and question them before you do? Amduscias is back, and he's claimed several people, including me."

Every single tree demon started giggling and checking their hair and breath when I asked if he could come. Why was I not surprised he even flirted with a fucking tree? He was a flirt, but he was loyal, I would give him that. He wouldn't have stuck around Scorchwood for so long if he had commitment issues.

The lead tree demon rustled his leaves.

"Okay, you can send for the handsome Duke now."

SERAFINA

Lady Godiva had nothing on me. I was sitting on a big, beautiful demonic unicorn in the middle of a forest in Hell. There was even this breeze going that kept blowing my hair back. I had Skoll's wolf at my right and a Vampire with their fangs out, ready to rip a throat to my left. To say I felt pretty fucking badass was an understatement.

I was trying to focus on the fact that if anyone happened upon us, we made a pretty impressive tableau instead of the fact that I was worried about Fergus. I already knew I was getting a unicorn ride because they were all worried about me. I knew we had to be quiet and alert because there could be snipers, but fuck me, I really needed to talk my stress out. Where was Fergus? He had been gone too long.

I let out the breath I was holding when I heard his voice in my head.

"The tree demons are on our side. They hate Gusion and have

subdued all the assassins. They like Amduscias, and I've managed to get them to hold off on killing them so they can be questioned, but tell Amduscias the tree demons think it's their right to kill the assassins."

I relayed the message to Amduscias telepathically, and I swear, the unicorn I was sitting on started laughing.

"Vagolin is their leader. If Gusion told his assassins to use that area of the forest, he's dumber than I thought. That particular grove of trees happened when a tree demon got together with a shadow demon. The children ended up with tree demon powers, but with a shadow demon attitude. They like picking fights. If Gusion weren't a Duke, they would have killed him by now. They are very territorial about their grove."

"Should Skoll shift back? We don't have clothes for him."

"No. Vagolin will like the display of power that I came in my demonic form. He'll respect you because I let you ride on my back. He'll want to see Skoll's wolf so he can size him up, and he'll want to check out Roman. And yes, every single tree demon will stare at Skoll's junk when he transforms back. Best not get too territorial on that one. I dated one of them briefly. It ended on suitable terms, and we are all friends. They like to look and comment, but they don't fish in other people's ponds if you get my meaning."

I let Skoll and Roman know we were moving and following Amduscias. I just enjoyed the ride. I'd never even ridden a horse before. There was something strangely erotic about riding Amduscias's unicorn. He jostled me in a certain way that was turning me on. Was this why so many girls were into horses when I was topside? Because if we weren't riding to a bunch of tree demons with nasty atti-tudes who were holding assassins hostage, I might have gotten off on this.

The tree demons were something else. I'm not sure what I was expecting, but if you had to picture demonic trees in your head, that was about it. They were tall and thin with glowing eyes and leaves for hair. This wasn't a dryad from Narnia. This was a fucking tree with arms, legs, and really sharp teeth. I had a feeling these weren't the kindly trees providing leaves for birth control.

They all started giggling when they saw Amduscias. I slid off his back, and he transformed into a man. He said he dated one of them, but they were all acting like he had a group thing going with all of them. A big scary one that must be Vagolin came over and clasped arms with him.

"You bring an impressive array with you, but you used to only keep the company of demons."

"Things change, Vagolin. We are all in danger. We need to find out which Dukes hired these men. They trespassed in your grove, so their death is yours, but we need to question them."

Vagolin gave a deep bow.

"Ask away. Any way we can assist. Ask the little fire elemental to keep her fire to herself."

I could kiss a little tree demon ass if it meant not starting a war with them. We were outnumbered, and it looked like they were about to rip that warlock's leg clean off. I bowed my head.

"I wouldn't dream of starting a fire in your grove."

"Good. The warlock with the snake tattoo is the leader. He was the one trampling through our grove barking orders. It'll be nice to see the master at work."

Amduscias clucked his tongue.

"And I don't have any of my good toys on me. Hello. What is your name?"

The warlock with the terrible snake tattoo on his neck just sneered at Amduscias. He started hocking like he was about to spit a loogie on his face, but Amduscias, punched him in the nose before he could finish. The warlock started choking.

"Let's not be uncivilized, okay?"

Charley skipped up to the front. She was more awake than I'd seen her in prison. It was like the fresh air in Hell had made her come alive. She was practically sparkling. She had on this trench coat at the execution, and she had pulled the vials she had given me out of it. She whipped the jacket open and looked like some witchy super spy when we saw her coat was lined with all kinds of potions.

"These were leftover from the execution. October and I prepared all of these in case Serafina wanted to get a little creative."

Charley told me a little about what Zepar had done to October and her coven. Zepar had slept his way through two covens in Hell, giving them all some awful rash. That was the real reason he was allowed to go topside. Bael would not let him until he had two covens ready to curse his cock. I hadn't had the time to fill Amduscias in on all of that.

"So, you gave Serafina potions to give syphilis and a tiny cock. What presents do you have for me today, Charley?" Amduscias asked.

"You keep that witch away from my cock," the warlock growled.

I swear, men and their cocks. Amduscias could have tortured him half to death, and he wouldn't have spilled who hired him. Threaten him with a tiny witch who could curse his cock, and he was ready to sing an entire opera. We could work with that. I didn't even know if this was true, but the warlock didn't have to know that.

"She's got a potion that will make your balls rot right off."

"I actually do," Charley said gleefully.

Okay, Charley was officially the coolest witch in Hell. We were going to have to hang out more when this was over.

"That is so cool," I said, holding up my hand for a high five.

Charley smacked my hand and grinned at the warlock.

"You're ruining my chance at freedom, asshole. I like it here, and you are fucking it up. You'd better talk, or I'll melt your balls off. I'll go through every single one of you until one of you talks."

"Yeah, you'll fit right in down here in Hell, Charley," Amduscias said.

"Just keep the testicle melting potion away from me, okay?" Roman said, adjusting his crotch.

Skoll finally changed back to a man and glared at the two shifters.

"You give us a terrible name."

Three female tree demons and two males started giggling and checking Skoll out.

"Is the wolf yours too, Amduscias?"

"Knock it off, Banaz. You can sense full well that Skoll has marked Serafina."

"I know. But he shares her. Does she share too?"

Skoll was preening under all the attention. Fucking wolf.

"She shares, but not with me. I don't want her to share me."

"So, I could get a piece of that sexy Vampire?" Banaz said.

What the fuck was wrong with these trees? They had seven assassins restrained with roots, we were trying to put down a rebellion in Hell, and they were trying to get laid. Roman just flashed her a bit of fang.

"I'm her mate too, but the only person I want to be shared with is Amduscias."

"I'm devoted to Serafina and Roman, Banaz," Amduscias said. "And before you ask, the Fae is loyal to her too."

Banaz just pouted.

"Lucky girl. Let's get on with the testicle melting. I'm getting bored."

One warlock who hadn't spoken finally decided to grace us with his voice.

"I'll talk. Zepar hired us, but he was always an asshole. Gusion offered us more money if we took care of the kings and then Zepar. It was nothing personal. It's just a job."

"What is your name?" Vagolin asked.

"Finn. Please, we were told this was a safe place to enter. We weren't told you lived here. If we knew, we wouldn't have come to this place. Gusion gave us bad intel. He was the one who didn't care about strangers and guns in your forest. Believe us, now that we know Gusion didn't care about you or us, we want him dead just as much as all of you seem to."

There was this quote I'd always remembered about there being no honor among thieves. My mates and I could all be viewed as bad guys. We killed people and liked it. I burned down many people's property and enjoyed the fuck out of watching it burn.

I guess there were two distinct types of villains in the world. There was us, who had our reasons for killing people. We were trying to make the world a better place by leveling the playing field. We knew how to play nice with others, and when it came down to brass tacks, I guess you could call us chaotic good.

Then you had the other spectrum of villains. You had the chaotic evil like Zepar and his cohorts. There was no loyalty and honor there. They stabbed their own friends in the back, and it wouldn't shock me if any of these people ate babies or something. They didn't care who they hurt as long as their futile plan worked. At least I had standards about who I murdered, and I didn't point my fire at someone just for money. That would just be uncouth.

"What do you say, Vagolin?" Amduscias asked.

What kind of deal was he trying to make? These were bad guys. They snuck into Hell to assassinate the kings. Let the tree demons do their thing. They didn't have any type of honor when it came to killing. It came down to the dollar amount someone was willing to pay. They probably pointed their guns at some innocent people and pulled the trigger with no remorse. If I wouldn't have set an entire grove of demons on fire, I would have just lit them all up.

"The one who confessed only. There's more to his story than this just being a job. He just doesn't want to say it in front of the others."

Amduscias just gave a curt nod.

"Very well. Proceed."

It was like this light switch of gore and mayhem went off. These tree demons didn't care about who they got blood on. Have you ever seen a shifter ripped apart by tree roots? It's about as graphic as a fire dragon exploding someone from inside their stomach. You just don't get as much burned bits on your hair.

I wiped the blood off my face.

"Seriously?"

"Thanks for the snack," Roman said, licking his lips. "The shifter is not half bad."

Skoll just groaned.

"Only you would try to eat blood spatter."

"What? It was just going to go to waste."

"Enough," Vagolin said. "Now, Finn. You were lying when you said this was just a job to you. What did you mean?"

"I didn't take this job for the money. I never do. I was told I was helping overthrow a corrupt monarchy, but the more I met with Zepar, the less I thought he should take over. Gusion offered an alternative and seemed like a better option until I realized he sent us here, not caring what would happen to us or the trees. I'm sure he was hoping we would kill the tree demons for him."

Well, maybe I was glad I didn't set him on fire now if he wasn't lying. The roots holding him disappeared into the earth. They gently lowered Finn to the ground. He had been held in the air and stretched within an inch of his life for who knows how long. He collapsed as soon as his feet hit the ground.

Charley rushed to a fellow warlock and started to heal him with her magic. Every eye was on him.

"We spared your life because we sensed you were different. That can change at any minute. We are in the middle of a rebellion here. We aren't going to pay you a fucking dime. Will you help us end this, then get the fuck out of Hell?" Amduscias asked.

Finn just gave us all this painful grin as Charley continued to try to heal him.

"Are you kidding? I was lied to by two different demons. My kill record is spotless. There isn't a single innocent person on it. I take a lot of fucking pride in that. I'd be happy to help you take him out and leave here with no money."

Amduscias clapped his hands.

"Good. Then I don't have to kill you. We've dallied here long enough. I need to check in, then we join the fight."

SERAFINA

I had never been in a war before. Fuck, I tried to avoid fistfights in public because I didn't want attention to be brought to me and my activities. I watched too much television for a simple battery charge to link me to arson and murder. I wasn't counting on the fucking warden of Scorchwood framing me so she could get me pregnant. I wasn't counting on Zepar and all these Dukes being power-hungry life ruiners who were going to lead me to this point in my life.

Amduscias was on the phone with Bael trying to get an update. Thankfully, he'd finally figured out the wonders of speakerphone, so we didn't have to stand around trying to figure out what the fuck was going on.

"I knew you could handle it, Amduscias. Agares surrendered once his legions turned on him. I still don't know why Saleos is a part of this, but he agreed to surrender only if he could have an audience with the entire court to say his peace before he gets his punishment. I've granted him that. Gusion is the last problem to deal with."

"Well, all his assassins are dead except the one that turned on him. Surely, he'll go quietly when he realizes this mission of his is doomed."

"You know he won't. Gusion knows he's going to die. He's never been the kind of demon to admit his mistakes. Gusion is going to force our hand and try to take as many people with him as he can on the way out. He's holed up in his dungeon, and he's already brought his baboon out."

"What's so scary about a monkey?" I asked.

"You won't be so cavalier when you see his teeth and he flings feces at you," Bael said.

"Ew. Why is a Duke of Hell flinging shit at people?"

"Because he has to get people confused before he can have the upper hand with the demonic form he was dealt and there's no better way to do that than a face full of shit. I used to have a pet monkey. She had to be trained not to do that," Bael said.

Skoll was pretty grumpy. Getting objectified by a bunch of trees had its limits when we were all covered in blood and gore. Skoll was always extremely clean. I used to think he took so many showers in Scorchwood because he enjoyed showing off naked, but that was just him. He showered several times a day in Hell and loved soaking in the bathtub. It was rather nice to take a bath with him.

"Tell us how to kill him before we get shit on us. I'm already covered in blood. I have to draw the line somewhere."

"I can get him with an arrow," Fergus said.

"I can just shoot him in the head," Finn said.

"I can fling a spell at him to immobilize him," Charley said.

Well, fuck. Everyone had a way to kill him but me. My fire wouldn't work on him, and that had never happened to me before. I never learned to shoot a gun because I didn't need to. Fuck, I had a fire dragon and could set things on fire with my mind, and that was useless right now. How did that manage to happen?

"What is the layout of his dungeon?" I asked.

"Dungeons are private," Amduscias said. "I haven't been to every dungeon in Hell."

"I haven't seen his dungeon since the last time he upgraded," Bael said. "There's no telling what kind of weapons he may have stockpiled down there. We shouldn't portal in. We'll have to go through the front door," Bael said.

Hell torture dungeons had front doors? We'd portalled in every time we'd visited one. I was starting to think that was the only way in. I had a feeling they were underground, but I never actually saw a door to any of these things before. I thought the location was this big secret, and you only wanted a personal invitation to watch the torture or play in the bedroom portion of one.

I raised my hand like I was back in class with the nuns. I had a question, but I didn't really want to speak because I had a feeling the question would get me some dirty looks. I didn't think anyone in Hell would judge me, but I didn't think they wanted me knowing all the ins and outs of their torture dungeons.

"Won't he be guarding the door? I didn't even know dungeons had doors. If it's not safe to portal, won't it be just as unsafe to go through the front door? How do we know he doesn't have some secret sniper down there with him? He already snuck seven of them in."

"The elemental is right," Finn said. "Is there a way for me to get a vantage point in there?"

"We design hell dungeons to be secure. The only way in is by portal or the access code on the front door—Scratch that. We can't use the front door. Everyone is supposed to report their codes to the kings in case we need to get in there, but Gusion will count on us knowing it and will have changed it. We have no choice but to portal in."

"Some other guys brought tear gas, but no masks. They intended to throw it into the fight and pick people off. I don't kill that way, but if you have a mask, I could gas him, then get him out," Finn said.

Charley was eyeing Finn like she wanted to rip his clothes off and fuck him. Finn was showing off for her. I knew he was helping us because of some assassin's honor code, but he was trying to impress Charley. Good for them. Was our little witch friend going to find love? If not, was she at least going to have some hot sex?

"We have no such thing here," Bael said. "I have three heads in my demonic form, and I can't be killed unless you kill all three. The portal will be hazy when I step through. I'll go first. I want Finn behind me with his gun and Fergus with his arrows. If you see him before he sees us, shoot to kill. We don't need some lengthy torture sessions and public execution. I can just put his head on a pike in the town square. He's the last hold out in his rebellion, and I want him dead."

Fergus and Finn were all ready to charge through that portal and take out an errant Duke, but why did it have to be Fergus? He didn't have three heads. If Gusion shot him, he would bleed out or die. I liked nothing about this plan, but I knew better than to say anything.

Fergus was a warrior and a Fae hero. I wouldn't have wanted anyone telling me they didn't want me to fight, and I wouldn't do that to Fergus either. I also knew better than to say to him I wanted to be there standing right next to him when the portal opened. I wasn't stupid.

Fergus and I always fought together. From the moment he let himself be known to me, we'd always taken the bad guys out as a team. My greatest weapon was gone. I didn't think a terrible attitude and Krav Maga would beat a gun if Gusion had one.

I wasn't even sure if it would beat a demonic baboon.

FERGUS

I used to live for the heat of battle. I was young and stupid. I died before I could outgrow that. When I was younger, I would have been foolish enough to be excited about portalling into the unknown. Everyone knew it was dangerous. The older, smarter Fae knew not to do it unless you absolutely had to. The younger Fae would have done it for a thrill.

I wasn't nineteen anymore. This wasn't exciting. I had someone I wanted to come home to now and everything to lose if this went wrong. Still, I was a soldier and a guardian. I'd been on the front lines before, and this was no different. I fought for my king before. I fought for my Ena now, and I would do everything in my power to kill Gusion and live through this.

When Bael brought out his demonic form, I was a little less worried about standing behind him with my arrows. I guess he didn't get to be king of Hell for nothing. Especially when he said one of his demonic powers was to make us all invisible. Couldn't he have said all that before? He dropped it in passing like he was talking about the weather. Having that power might seem minor to him, but it was quite significant to me. It would keep my Ena safe.

Bael mutated and got even more prominent when he changed to his demonic form. The face I knew and had been talking to this entire time was still there, but he had a colossal toad head on one shoulder and a black cat with red eyes on the other. He was much bigger than I was, and I was reasonably large for a Fae.

I couldn't feel it when he did it. I didn't even know it happened. I could still see everyone in our party clear as day.

Bael just clapped his hands.

"Is everyone ready to go through the portal and end this?"

My Ena questioned him. She questioned everything and for a good reason. It kept her alive this long. It kept her out of prison until she managed to get under Warden Skinner's radar. She just asked what we were all thinking.

"Um, not to question your demonic powers, your holiness, but I can still see all of us."

All three of Bael's heads started laughing.

"I like your woman, Amduscias. Of course, you can all see each other. If you couldn't, you could kill each other. That's the beauty of it. You can see each other, but no one else can see you."

Serafina just narrowed her eyes at him.

"I'm only trusting that because you're the king of Hell, and you've been on our side this far. I usually trust my eyes. I'm not used to demon powers."

"If he has a gun, he can still hit someone. He'll be firing

blindly. He knows this is one of my powers, but I doubt he thinks I would have come myself. It would be best to keep moving once the portal opens. Spread out and get a vantage point to attack. In fact, you should probably duck as soon as the portal opens. We don't normally fight with guns down here, but we also don't start rebellions to overthrow the monarchy, so expect anything."

When Bael said expect anything, I thought I was prepared when the portal opened. Nothing prepared me for a demonic baboon holding an AR-15. I didn't even let my arrow fly. I grabbed Serafina and hit the floor. Gusion was like a madman.

"So, it's you, Bael. I thought you didn't do your own dirty work!" Gusion yelled.

I looked around. We were all hiding behind some implement of torture, and Gusion had no idea where we were. He was looking around wildly, but he wasn't shooting. He was trying to save bullets.

"Why do this, Gusion? Hell would never follow you. Hell would never have followed any of you in this plot."

Gusion raised his gun in the air and fired it like some drunk redneck at a barbeque.

"Because I'm fucking bored! We all had our reasons, but you fucked me over. You kept denying my request to live topside. I'm a Duke. I should be able to do what I want and go where I want."

I had my arrow aimed right at his left eye. I had a shot, and Serafina was safe. I could see Finn had a chance too. Were we really going to let them have a conversation while we sat down here in a torture dungeon with a baboon with an assault rifle? What was the protocol here? Was this a Kanye West thing, and we were supposed to let him finish?

Finn knew the score. He met my eye from behind his

metal gurney. The longer Bael talked, the sooner Gusion could pinpoint a location from his voice. One of us would have to take a shot. Finn gave me a nod, and he didn't have to say a word. Gusion could have his Kanye West moment, but he wasn't getting that gun while he did it.

I changed my aim from his eye to his hand. He still had the gun on his hip with one hand holding it upwards like some movie poster. Gusion howled, and the weapon clattered to the floor when my arrow buried itself in his hand. Roman used his Vampire speed to grab the gun, but that wasn't exactly the standard model when Roman was last topside. He held it by his pointer finger and thumb like he didn't want to touch it and just brought it to Finn to deal with it.

Gusion was still holding his hand and cursing. There wasn't much civil conversation to be had with an arrow sticking out of his hand, but we could have all been shot if we let Bael and Gusion work this out with his gun.

Apparently, Bael had heard enough too and had just been waiting for us.

"His hand? Someone get him in the head and end this. Fergus, you should know better."

I should know better? He was the demon trying to talk to a baboon with an assault rifle. How was I supposed to know he didn't really want to have that conversation?

Finn was trying to aim as Gusion crashed around the room, holding his hand. He couldn't get a clear headshot because Gusion's head was bowed over his hand. I couldn't get an arrow in his chest either because of how he was cradling his hands and hopping around the room.

Finn just stood.

"Let's light him up. Eventually, he'll die."

I jumped to my feet. I was a quick shot. I was taught

archery by the best. I got five arrows in him, and Finn shot him countless times before he finally fell over dead. Bael stepped over the corpse and kicked it.

Was that it? Was this finally over, and could we start making a home down here? Apparently not.

"Two Dukes down. We still have two more Dukes to deal with. Right this way. I don't want to dally."

Two more seemed like a lifetime.

AMDUSCIAS

What an utterly petty reason for joining Zepar. As far as temper tantrums went, Gusion's was the most extreme I'd seen in Hell. Zepar was greedy. He really intended to take over Hell. I still had no idea what had gotten into Saleos and Agares, but Gusion was just bored and looking to cause trouble because he wasn't getting his way. What a stupid reason to die. He was older than I was. Did he just tire of everything and decide to go out with a bang?

I guess we would never know. Gusion was dead, just like he wanted. Could he just not bring himself to pull the trigger on his own if he really did have nothing left to live for, or did he just want to fuck everyone else over on the way out? He accomplished one thing. His name would always be remembered. Not in a good way, but people would talk about Gusion for centuries.

Bael wanted this to be over just as much as we did. He

opened up a portal to his sitting room and starting barking orders into his cell phone. Portals started opening everywhere as the rest of the demon court started coming in. No one looked ruffled or bloodied. None of the legions put up much of a fight. Saleos and Agares surrendered. Gusion was the only one who wanted to take as many people out with him as he could.

The seven kings all took their thrones in Bael's court. The thrones were up on a high platform so they could look down on us. There was a slightly lower platform with benches for the Dukes. The accused would have to stand below us, and there were seats for witnesses and audience members. As much as I wanted them with me, everyone I claimed would have to sit in the audience.

I squeezed Serafina's hand and touched Roman's shoulder.

"Take a seat on the front row. I'll be up there with the other Dukes. Hopefully, this will be over soon."

"What are we doing?" Serafina asked.

"Holding a trial. We all know they are guilty, but this needs to happen. It would give us all clarification if we knew why they did this. Gusion and Zepar would have been given public trials after we had time to torture information out of them, but they made it, so that wasn't a possibility."

"Is it going to be long and drawn out like topside trials?"

I smiled at her.

"Not unless something has changed since I've been away."

I took my seat. I was hoping they brought Saleos out first. I didn't take him for joining a rebellion at all. We were never close, but it was always because I was never serious enough for him. Saleos took his role as part of Hell's monarchy quite seriously and tried to get involved in all the decision making.

Most of the other Dukes didn't. We were spoiled and only did the bare minimum. We fought when asked and did the duties assigned to us, but never anything more. Maybe more than just me realized the only reason we had our positions and cushy lifestyles was that we happened to be spat from the fires of Hell. I went through a point in my life where I didn't take my Dukedom seriously because the only reason I had it was because of how I was born. Saleos was never like that, and he thought I should be a lot more serious about it.

Agares was brought out first, and I knew what he was doing. He came out in his demonic form instead of the face we all knew. His demonic form was a feeble old man riding a crocodile. He wanted us to feel sorry for him, and there was no fucking way that was happening. The kings weren't stupid. They knew exactly what he was doing too.

"You know the rules, Agares. No demonic forms allowed in court. Change back right this instant," Bael barked.

I'd never seen Bael this angry before, and I'd pissed him off plenty of times. I'd never attempted to overthrow and murder him before, but I got up to some shit in my younger days. The rest of the kings knew better than to try to talk when he was this mad. When Bael was pissed off, it was best not to speak unless he asked you a direct question and permitted you to speak.

Agares must be extremely stupid because Bael looked like he was ready to explode, and he didn't immediately drop his demonic form. He prostrated himself across his stupid crocodile and started begging.

"Please, your most gracious majesty—"

"Get off the fucking crocodile and change now!"

"Yes, your majesty, if you would just—"

"Did I stutter? I swear on my left nut if I am looking at your demonic form when I open my eyes after I blink, you will lose both of yours in the middle of this court."

Agares had never been the brightest demon, and Bael wasn't joking about castrating him. He'd probably cut the balls off the crocodile too if he could find them. That was just Bael when he was mad. Any other demon wouldn't have been dumb enough to rock out to their trial going full demon, then refused to drop it when Bael commanded them to.

I wouldn't mind witnessing a castrating. I was currently covered in blood. At least it wasn't exploded warlock this time. None of us were given a chance to shower before the trial. My entire group was splashed with blood. Vagolin had never been very clean when it came to killing people. It was starting to dry on my skin and get sticky. I wished Agares would just shut the fuck up and drop his demonic form so we could get on with it. Either that or Bael would just kill him.

Maybe Agares wasn't totally stupid. He changed back before Bael lost it. He was small for a demon with white-blonde hair and a weak chest. He decided to prostrate himself again, and he tried the begging route again. Maybe he really was dumber than a rock.

"I don't want to hear anything out of your mouth except for a reason why you joined this stupid rebellion."

"Solron. Please, sir."

Bael had fire dancing in his eyes.

"You'd better be *very* careful about what you say next, Agares."

"I want her, but she won't give me the time of day. Zepar said I could have her when we won," Agares whined.

Well, that was fucking stupid. I hadn't known her long, but I already knew she'd kill him as soon as they were alone if someone tried to gift her to him. Solron wasn't taking that lying down. She stood in the back of the court.

"You utter shit!"

Solron must have Bael wrapped around her little finger because he gave her this adoring look.

"So, all this for a woman. You must be dumber than I thought. You'll die by her hand. Solron, you have my permission to torture him as long as you like and kill him. Have fun, my love."

Solron skated up to the front in a strange pair of skates. They didn't need to be used on ice, and they weren't made of bone. They had weird wheels in a straight line on the bottom, and she had a piece of candy on a stick in her mouth. She was still a young demon, and she was wearing her hair in pigtails like a child. Agares was looking at her like a lost puppy dog. If he couldn't have her, he would take getting killed by her.

"Let's go, shit for brains," she said, yanking him off to a shadow where she could take him to Bael's dungeon.

Bael steepled his fingers and sighed.

"Bring me Saleos."

I leaned forward and rested my elbows on my knees. This was something I wanted to hear. Saleos wouldn't have done this for greed, boredom, or a woman. Something else got him to join this rebellion, and I was dying to know what.

Saleos must have a death wish too because he came out in his demonic form as well. Like Zepar, he was a soldier. He gave Bael a curt nod, then dropped it. Saleos was a large demon, even without his demonic form. He was much bigger than I was when I wasn't going full demon. He went down on one knee and bowed his head.

"Why, Saleos? Out of everyone, it makes no sense with you."

Saleos raised his face, and there was pain behind his gray eyes.

"It makes sense if you think about it."

Bael took in a hissing breath.

"Still?"

"It's always been about that."

"You realize I can't let this go. You have to die for this."

"I know. I made my point. Now, I expect things to change. If a Duke was willing to die for the smoke and flame demons, then things need to change. They need to be protected. Witches and warlocks shouldn't be able to summon them. I don't care what it takes. No one should be able to summon a demon anymore. Stop training them to go out and punish the witches and warlocks after the fact. Stop them from summoning us in the first place."

Bael looked sad. I had no idea what happened that Saleos took up the cause of the flame and smoke demons, but I agreed with him. Something needed to be done. But why had it gotten to the point that he felt the need to rebel to make his opinion known?

"Why didn't you come to me?" Bael asked.

"I did—several times. You kept putting forth ideas, but never any solutions. I want you to remember my death. I want it to stop, Bael. Don't make this rebellion mean noth-ing. Stop our people from getting hurt."

Bael stood.

"You have my word, Saleos. Your death will have mean-ing. I will make it quick. I want this over. Solron is having her fun with Agares. Saleos will be executed privately, and then I want us all to put this behind us. We will meet in the morning to discuss measures to put in place so this doesn't happen again and to keep our demons safe from summoning. It will take time, but this is Saleos's last wish, and I will honor it."

Armed demons came to take Saleos away. I didn't want to see him executed. I didn't need to view it. He died because he felt like Bael wasn't listening to him. He joined this rebellion for what he thought were principled reasons. He knew he would lose, and he knew he would die. He just wanted his moment in front of the court to have his say.

In a way, I admired him. He died for what he believed in. I decided I would take part in the discussions to keep our demons safe from summoning. It was his last wish. We might not have been close, but I would honor it.

Bael stood and smoothed his clothes down.

"I would like Amduscias and his crew at my house for dinner. After they have showered and changed, of course."

I knew that was coming. I also hoped to find out more about what caused Saleos to take up this cause. It was common for Bael to call a dinner with Dukes after battle. As much as I wanted this to be over and make Hell home for my friends, we weren't there yet.

SERAFINA

I was feeling left out of this little Hell victory celebration. I didn't get to kill a single bad guy. I only got to give Zepar syphilis before a sniper took him out. I was still mad about that, by the way. I doubted Bael would put me in charge of any more executions, and even if he did, it wouldn't have the same meaning as Zepar. My heart wouldn't be as into killing that person as it was for Zepar. It wasn't like I could just go find another evil person in Hell and kill them to make myself feel better either. I was pretty sure they would look down on that here.

I stepped through the portal into Amduscias's bedroom. I had blood spattered all over my face and clothes from when those tree demons ripped those assassins apart. That was pretty gory. The noises it made as their limbs ripped from their bodies was something I probably wouldn't forget for a while. I wanted a shower and a nap, but we still had to do dinner at Bael's.

Amduscias growled at me.

"You and Roman look so sexy with the spoils of battle all over you."

"I didn't even get to punch anyone," I pouted.

"Hey, you gave a Duke of Hell syphilis in public. No one else can make that claim. I know you didn't get to finish, but you still humiliated him before he died."

"It would have been better if I got to give him a micro cock first."

Fergus pulled me into a bloody hug.

"She always gets cranky when something final happens to a bad guy, and she didn't get to do it."

"*You* got to kill a bad guy."

"And now I'm glad this is over, and you are safe."

"Can we take a shower?" Skoll asked. "This blood is getting gross."

"Speak for yourself," Roman said.

"Roman, this is like the time those shifters started throwing food all over the cafeteria, and you pitched a fit you got oatmeal all over you for the rest of us," Skoll said.

"Oh, come on. It's so not the same."

"You got plastered in our food and didn't like it. We feel the same about being covered in yours."

"I think we can all admit blood is way tastier than that shitty oatmeal."

They could sit there and argue this all day. I didn't want to be covered in lousy oatmeal, and I didn't want to be covered in blood either.

"Let's just get in the shower. Group shower?"

"We don't have time for a quickie," Amduscias said. "Bael will expect us to be back at his place for dinner soon. We can have our post-battle nookie session after dinner."

All I had was dream nookie with my dragon. I hadn't

gotten to enjoy him now that he was real. It was sexy as fuck watching him riddle Gusion with arrows, and I didn't even get a make-out session because Bael was ordering us all through the portal back to his house. Bael might be the supreme king of Hell, but he was turning into a real cock-blocker.

"I'm scrubbing her back and washing her hair," Fergus said. "All of you have gotten a shower or bath with her. I haven't."

Skoll clapped him on the back.

"I'm sorry they ruined your big moment, Fergus. It's nice to meet you in person finally. I just want to get all this blood off of me."

Amduscias got his look on his face and started batting his eyelashes.

"Well, if Fergus is washing Serafina, can Roman and I wash each other?"

I swear they were trying to kill me. Fergus scrubbing my body while watching Roman and Amduscias soap each other up? And we couldn't have shower sex? Kill me right now.

I think everyone wanted the blood off them except Roman, who I believe was getting off on it. We all went to the bathroom silently and started stripping off our clothes. Amduscias had this fantastic bathroom. It was like whoever designed it planned for shower orgies. There was easily enough room for all of us and showerheads all over the place so we could get clean.

I stepped under the scalding water, and I honestly didn't know what I wanted to look at. Fergus, Skoll, Roman, or Amduscias. Fergus didn't leave me much of a choice. He got behind me with a loofah and started scrubbing my back. Skoll was behind me. He liked to sing in the shower, and he had an excellent voice. I had no idea what song it was other than old.

My eyes were plastered on Roman and Amduscias. They were hot, naked, and covered in soap. Their hands were everywhere, and they were both erect. I knew I would have issues with this. Fergus wasn't just soaping my back. He was massaging the soap in. I leaned back against him and rested my head against his shoulder. He reached around me and started soaping my breasts. We could have a little quickie, right?

I mean, Roman and Amduscias were concentrating pretty hard on soaping up each other's cocks. My mouth was watering. I wanted to touch everyone in this shower so badly. I nearly screamed when Fergus pinched my nipple and removed his hands.

He started working the shampoo into my hair and scratching my scalp. Roman was stroking Amduscias's cock with his head thrown back and his mouth forming this big O. God, that was so hot. Skoll was right behind me singing away like there wasn't a sexy demon and Vampire jerking each other off covered in soap.

Fergus grabbed the showerhead off the wall and started rinsing my hair. I was dancing on my feet because I was so fucking turned on. I lost it when Roman and Amduscias were soap-free, and Amduscias fell on his knees and started sucking Roman off.

"Well, shit," Fergus said as he rinsed the conditioner out of my hair.

Fergus slammed the showerhead back on the wall and wrapped his arms around my waist. One hand went to my breasts, and the other found my clit. He started nibbling on my neck. My eyes were glued to Amduscias's head, bobbing on Roman's cock. Roman's eyes were glowing red, and he was watching Amduscias too until he realized I was enjoying the show. He started watching Fergus finger me.

Skoll was oblivious to all of this. I could still hear him singing away behind us. He kept singing even when I let out this huge moan. I was like a live wire. This needed to be a quickie, and we all knew that. Fergus was practically an expert on getting me off by now.

I grabbed his forearm and dug my nails in. Fergus had this deep, sexy voice, and the Fae accent sounded a lot like an Irish accent. He got right next to my ear.

"I will ravish you later, my Ena."

"Me too," Roman growled.

I thought Skoll wasn't paying attention, but he finally stopped singing briefly.

"Me three. Don't think I can't tell what's going on over there."

I'm sure Amduscias would have said something too, but he was deep throating Roman. This was it. It was almost over. We just had to get through dinner at Bael's and wrap up a few loose ends. Then, this would all be over, and we would make this our home. I could get to know Charley better and maybe make friends with Solron and the other elementals here.

First, I had to finish my little shower orgy.

ROMAN

I was *bored* with demon plots and Hell revolutions. And prison was fucking boring. Sure, it was exciting at first, but it got old fast. I wanted more shower sex, and Serafina said there were a lot more movies with the little green man that talked funny. I wanted to watch more videos with him in it. I also wanted to just sit down and read. They didn't even give us a library in Scorchwood.

That shower sex was fucking hot. And now that I'd had hot showers, I was furious about all the cold showers I had to take in prison. If I had known showers could be hot, maybe I would have gotten up the nerve to invite Amduscias or at least told him how I felt.

I wanted more sex. I wanted to sink my fangs into Amduscias and Serafina and get blood everywhere while we all fucked. That wasn't possible. I had to get dressed after my shower and go have dinner with the king of Hell. I was trying not to be a pouty bastard as I stepped through the portal to his sitting room.

We weren't alone. Finn was there with Charley. I saw why Bael hadn't booted him out of Hell after he helped kill Gusion. Finn and Charley were into each other. I squealed like a woman and ran to her. I picked Charley up off the floor and spun her around. Maybe this dinner wasn't so bad. I set her down to whisper in her ear.

"I think you *like* him, Charley."

"I do. Don't embarrass me, Roman. I still have some of that microcock potion."

I sat her down and tapped my index finger to my nose. We all followed Bael into the dining room. I hadn't realized Eiltan and Ior were invited until they popped out of the shadows like some crazy Vampire movie Serafina showed me. I had no idea who Count Dracula was or why they made a movie about him, but we just *did not* act like that. I wouldn't mind wearing a cape, though. That part was cool.

What were we doing about Eiltan? Were we still killing him? It was Warden Skinner's fault Scorchwood was so shitty, and her coven was the one who framed all those elementals. What were we doing about that coven too? I had questions. I wanted this to be over, but this was way bigger than I imagined. I think I liked shit better when Eiltan was the only bad guy. Now, I wasn't even sure if he deserved to die and a Vampire who didn't know how he felt was just bound to up and kill someone.

I didn't know how to feel, and I didn't know what to do at their appearance, so I did nothing. He wasn't my father, and this wasn't up to me. If Serafina wanted him dead, I'd rip his head off for her, but I'd never kill her father without her permission. I'd never try to tell her she needed my permission to murder anyone, but this was her father. She'd probably be furious at me if I just up and killed him right here, and that wasn't what she wanted.

He looked like he didn't know if she still wanted to kill him either. He had this tense look on his face like she would burst into flames, grab the nearest weapon off the wall, cut his heart out, and eat it. That would be fucking hot if she did.

I think we were all surprised when she smiled at him instead of up and killed him.

"I'm glad you're here. How was the battle topside?"

So, we weren't killing Eiltan. Duly noted. Unless she was playing with him. Maybe she wanted to eat first, and then we would be murdering Eiltan after dessert?

"I decided not to kill him, Roman. Are you okay with that?"

"Yeah, I just needed to know where we stood. No murdering Eiltan at dinner. Got it."

I was glad we'd shared so much blood, and she could feel I was so fucking confused right now to reach out to me telepathically. I'm sure I would have said something totally offensive at dinner to one of the different groups here, not knowing what we were doing with this Fae prince. I was chill now. Relaxed. I knew what was going on. We were having dinner with her father, and we *weren't* going to murder him at some point.

We all took our places at the table. I always hated the seating arrangements at Bael's. I didn't get to sit next to Serafina or Amduscias. I was stuck next to Fergus and Skoll, or last time, I was next to some stuffy king. I wanted to play footsie under the table, and Skoll wouldn't have appreciated it like Serafina and Amduscias would have. Eiltan and Ior were placed directly across from Serafina and to Bael's left.

Were we going to talk about it, or were we seriously going to sit here and wait until the food was brought out?

Not talking things out was why people got constipated. This was true for everyone, not just Vampires. Holding all that in was just asking for trouble. Bael was sitting there, sipping his wine like he wanted to be backed up for weeks. Ior finally spoke like he knew he'd be sitting on the toilet praying if he didn't get this all out.

"The topside battle was quite easy. When they saw an entire Fae army, they weren't foolish. Zepar promised them a Fae army as backup, but when they realized our weapons were pointed at them, they stopped. Some ran, some asked what was going on. We only had to kill a few of them. All of them hated Zepar. Some just thought they would still get paid or information would get released if they didn't carry out their task."

Bael let out this huge sigh and signaled to his staff to start bringing the food out. Honestly, I was starving. Amduscias gave me an epic blow job, but I didn't get to bite him and eat. I could go for some sweet blood, and I had no idea people just lined up to donate it now. I'd still prefer biting Serafina and Amduscias. There was nothing like sinking your fangs in and feeling the blood spurting in your throat, but I could be fancy at dinner and drink it from a goblet.

"I hear things went sideways here," Eiltan said.

"To put it mildly," Bael said. "Zepar wasn't working alone, and one of his comrades intended to betray him. Gusion had already snuck his assassins in. The Dukes and the assassins are all dead except Finn here, who helped. The last item we need to deal with is Warden Skinner's coven."

Well, fuck. I thought they had already been dealt with. I guess I couldn't blame Bael for not dealing with them. He had a revolt on his hands. But even so, I wanted more fucking and biting and fewer witch covens and wicked demons. There was only room for one naughty devil in my life.

"Can I go and finally kill someone?" Serafina asked.

Bael just gave her a gentle smile.

"Of course. You can kill all of them as far as I'm concerned, but please remember, no killing in Hell after this. We have rules here."

Serafina looked positively giddy.

"Go out with a bang, right?"

"Bael?" Amduscias said. "Why was Saleos so concerned about demon summoning?"

"It's a sad story. Saleos was set to marry a flame demon. As you know, we don't control who gets called when a witch or warlock tries to summon a demon. Unfortunately, someone tried to summon a demon during their wedding, and his bride was called in the middle of the ceremony. It was then we learned she was pregnant. By the time we found her, she was already dead."

Well, if that wasn't the saddest fucking thing I'd ever heard. I was just imagining someone taking Serafina from me at our wedding. I would kill them. Yeah, I'd even try to take over Hell for that. Why *wasn't* Hell doing more to protect their demons from summoning?

"Wiping out the knowledge to summon demons will be impossible, but you can't do it without certain ingredients," Finn said. "The hardest one to find is the Bitter Woundwort. It's almost impossible to find anywhere. Only specialty shops have it now, and it's grown in greenhouses in certain countries. Demon summoning is pretty much the only thing that herb is used for. Wipe that out and no more demon summoning."

"I'll be damned," Amduscias said. "The assassin has more use than just shooting things."

"We do still need to figure out what to do with you," Bael said. "You too, Charley. You have two choices. You can both stay in Hell, and Charley can claim Finn. Or, we can pull some strings, and you can both live topside. If you both stay in Hell, Finn would have to change jobs. We don't have assassins in Hell."

I saw Finn take Charley's hand, and I tried not to squeal again. It was just so fucking cute. I wanted to frame them and keep them at Amduscias's place.

"We didn't know if I would be allowed to stay here. I don't have to be an assassin. I think I'd like to be a coven member, and I'm good with my hands. I'd like to work in construction here if you'll actually let me stay."

Bael clapped his hands.

"Good. Then, it's settled. Finn will stay here with Charley. Now, there is just the matter of Serafina and her family."

"What about it?"

"The cure will be ready in the morning," Ior said. "We would like you to come back to the Fae realm with us as part of the victory team. You can also help us introduce some new laws and get rid of some old ones. We are opening the portal and getting rid of the laws about killing halflings. We would like you to be an ambassador for the halflings since you won't be our princess."

Serafina started choking at the word princess. Fergus had to smack her on the back.

"I didn't think anyone wanted me for a princess."

"Well, you're the firstborn of the prince, so you're next in line. There's never been a halfling on the throne, but there's never been one in the line of succession before. If you want it, just say so. If not, Eiltan here will have to get to work producing an heir."

Now, it was Eiltan that was choking. That was the marvelous thing about blood. It didn't get stuck in your throat like food. Sure, it could go down wrong, but you couldn't choke to death on it.

"I don't think I could rule an entire realm, but I will be your ambassador until you fire me. Which you will. Probably within a week."

Eiltan and Ior just laughed.

"I'm sure you'll be fine, my dear."

"We're going back tomorrow? What about the witches?"

"The witches are holed up in a castle in Romania. They think we don't know about it, but they all fled when Skinner went out of contact. It's pretty remote. You could show up and burn the thing down for all I care," Bael said.

Serafina's eyes lit up.

"Can we burn some witches before we go to the Fae realm?"

"Only because they are nasty witches. We'll leave after lunch."

"Are my mates welcome in the Fae realm?"

"Of course. The Fae should get used to other supernatural beings."

Well, I guess I was going to the Fae realm. We just needed to kill some witches first. I hoped we still got our orgy tonight.

SERAFINA

I was glad to see my family at dinner, which was weird because up until a few weeks ago, I didn't know they existed, and a few days ago, I was plotting how I would murder them. I got this weird feeling even if I still wanted to kill my father, he'd just sit there and let me for some fucked up reason. It would only take all the fun out of it if he just sat there and took it. My heart just wasn't into it anymore. My poor, fucked up black heart wanted to get to know him now—traitorous bastard.

Bael finally dismissed us, and I had no idea where they were staying. My father wanted to come with us when we took down the witches. I guess he wanted to bond with me over burning some nasty people alive? This was my last hurrah, and I needed to make it enjoyable. Elemental Batwoman couldn't come out and play in Hell unless Bael permitted me. He'd know it was me if people started cropping up burned to a crisp. Maybe Hell was a place she wasn't needed anyway.

"Where are you staying?" I asked.

I hoped it was somewhere good because I didn't really want to invite them back to Amduscias's place. Sure, I wanted to spend more time with them and get to know them, but I also intended to fuck myself silly tonight, and I didn't want my family anywhere near the house while that was going down.

"We are pulling a late night and sleeping here at Bael's. We will be working with the best demon doctors to make sure the remedy is ready for the Fae when we go back. I wouldn't worry about us. We have it handled and a place to sleep."

"Okay, good."

We just stood there, awkwardly. Did we hug now? Was this the part where normal families embraced? Shit. I was so bad at this. Did I even want a hug right now? That might make things even weirder. Yeah, I wasn't ready for hugs just yet. So, I just waved.

"Well, I'll see you tomorrow then."

Yeah, totally not awkward at all. Eiltan just gave me this nod like he understood and disappeared with Ior. I guess I liked that about him. He knew he fucked up, and he would not press shit with me. He'd probably even let me beat him up again if I wanted. I didn't really want to, I was just saying, if I wanted to, I probably had that option.

Fergus came up behind me and wrapped his arms around my waist. Now that he was here in the flesh, he smelled fucking amazing. It was more than just the body washes at Amduscias's. He smelled like a bonfire in the middle of nature underneath a clear sky.

"Are you okay, my Ena?"

"Can we go home? One day, I'll get used to having a family I don't want to kill."

Amduscias opened the portal back to his place.

"We can just talk or watch movies when we get back," he said.

"No way. I finally have all of you together, and this is almost over. I want to celebrate. We can talk about my daddy issues later."

Skoll joined my group hug.

"We could order takeout and watch more movies."

"We just stopped a hostile takeover of Hell. Tomorrow is my last day to do all my hobbies. I really do not want to talk about my feelings right now. I want to celebrate, and we just ate. I need this."

Skoll kissed my forehead.

"Then, let's go. We will always give you what you need."

Well, since they were tending to my needs and giving me everything I wanted, I had a few demands. Post battle orgies should be big. Everyone should get a fantasy.

"I want a Fergus Skoll sandwich. Then, I want to do kinky things to Roman with Amduscias."

Roman let out this little hiss.

"Stop telling her what she wants to do. I want to do kinky things too."

"Stop it, Roman, or I'll spank you," Amduscias said.

Roman just winked.

"Promise?"

"I'll spank you too if you want it, Roman," I said.

Roman moaned.

"Can we get out of this dining room now? Bael will be upset if he comes back in here, and I have a boner."

I grabbed Roman and pulled him through the portal. I needed a little of Roman's brand of psycho if I was retiring

Elemental Batwoman for good tomorrow. Roman had this playfulness about him I just needed. As soon as we stepped through and ended up in Amduscias's bedroom, I shoved him on the bed and tackled him. I rubbed my face in his neck.

"Does your boner feel safe now?"

"He'd feel better if you touched him."

"Roman, come here," Amduscias commanded. "Fergus had his moment ruined by Gusion's assassins. Wait your turn."

My eyes turned to Fergus. He didn't put his armor back on after our shower. No one knew his size before because they couldn't see him, so there were no clothes here for him just yet. He had to borrow from Skoll's closet because they were both huge. Have you ever seen a big, blonde Fae in leather trousers and their shirt unbuttoned just right? He was walking sex, but now I wanted him out of those clothes. He just stood there staring at me with those intense eyes of his.

I jumped off the bed and just flung myself at him. We'd kissed in dreams before, but now I was kissing him for real. I was kissing him like I'd been wishing the voice in my head could be a real boy so I could date him since I was eighteen. I'd wanted this for so long. After I realized that was him in my dream, I thought it was just me wishing again. When he told me this was possible, it was almost too good to be true.

But then we had to wait for this to be over. Well, it was over now, and Fergus was mine. He was here in the flesh, and no one would ever take him from me. He'd protected me and guided me for most of my adult life, but he could die now, and I would protect him too. If some snot-nosed Fae even tried to look at him wrong for loving me, I'd kill them. If he came back to the Fae realm with me when I was the halfling ambassador, my royal family better promise to keep him safe, or all bets were off.

I knew it was Skoll's shirt, and it felt expensive. If I ever found a way to earn money here, I'd replace it. I ripped the shirt open, and all the pearl buttons scattered to the floor. He helped me get the shirt off. I took a moment just to admire his broad chest and run my fingers down his washboard abs. They certainly broke the mold when they made Fergus.

We were both fumbling with the buttons and zipper on his trousers. I felt like screaming until the leather slid down his slim hips, and I finally got to see his erect cock. I'd seen it in dreams. I'd played with it in dreams. This was so much better.

I wanted to show Fergus how much I appreciated the voice in my head, so I fell on my knees and swallowed his cock. Fergus hissed and tangled his hands in my hair.

"I should be doing that to you, my Ena."

I didn't answer. My dreams had been all about him pleasing me. Everything he did was because I wanted to. I wanted Fergus to do things that gave him pleasure now that he had more options. I wanted to please him just as much as he'd devoted his life to me. I gave his balls a hard squeeze to let him know he would stand there, get a blowjob, and not worry about me for five minutes.

I thought he would let me finish, but Fergus was a little more dominant in person than he ever was in my dreams or in my head. I'd barely gotten started when he yanked me to my feet and destroyed my clothes, ripping them off.

I liked this side of Fergus. It was like all the fire that brimmed underneath the surface was coming out to play. It was just like in my dream where I could feel his fire mingling with mine. It was like a tingle on my skin. Fergus threw me on the bed and dove between my thighs. His oral skills were the same as in my dream, but Fergus was a little more out-of-control tonight. He seduced me the first night he did this. He was consuming me now.

It felt like little flames were dancing across my skin as his tongue flicked across my clit. I yanked his hair when he slid two fingers inside me. I was lucky no one in this room was offended by my potty mouth because I only seemed capable of screaming obscenities at the moment. I was shocked neither of us had set the bed on fire.

When I came, it was more intense than any of my dream sessions with Fergus. It was because he was a little out of control this time. He knew I loved him back, and that I was his now. He wasn't trying to seduce me or prove something like in my dreams. It was like all that pent-up frustration of being a voice in my head, and neither of us able to do anything about our feelings, finally just came to a head.

I was shaking. That was fucking intense. Fergus grinned at me from between my thighs.

"I believe a certain fire elemental wanted a Fae and wolf sandwich. Do you still want that, my Ena?"

Fuck, yes, I did.

SKOLL

I thought my wolf would hate another man in our bed, but oddly, we were both okay with Fergus. We understood where he was coming from. He kept her safe when we were in jail, and we didn't blame him for visiting her dreams and making himself known. If I had been her guardian and had been in her life that long, I probably wouldn't have been able to resist the temptation either.

The fact that I was even invited to their first time together after he became real said a lot about him. If it had been me, I probably would have booted everyone out of the room and demanded an entire night for myself. In fact, I wasn't sure we shouldn't be doing that now. I got my night with her when I was marking her. Fergus must be one generous fairy that he was sharing her tonight when I knew they both had something special planned when this happened.

But she wanted both of us, and I'd always give her what

she wanted. If she had just wanted to talk tonight, I would have done that too. Eventually, she would want to talk about her father, and I'd be waiting if she wanted an ear. If she just wanted to speak with Fergus because she was used to him, I'd deal with it. She had known him longer.

But, shit, did she look beautiful sprawled out on the bed with the flush of an orgasm on her breasts, even if I wasn't the one who gave it to her. I could still appreciate how beautiful my mate looked while she was enjoying some afterglow. That didn't mean I would not try to top what Fergus just gave her. My little fire elemental would be worn out tonight if she intended to take all of us because my wolf always had something to prove when other men were in her bed.

Fergus was still lying between her legs. I'd already rid myself of my clothing and was sprawled on a chair. Clothing was so restricting, and I already knew Bael would find it unacceptable if I showed up to dinner without a shirt on, so I wore this constricting garment that I couldn't wait to take off when we got home. If we were all having sex, it was pointless to keep my trousers on too. Plus, I loved it when Serafina took a peek when I was walking around naked.

"How do you want this to go, my Ena?"

"Well, Skoll needs to get off the chair and join us."

I perked up and jumped to my feet. She didn't need to ask me to her bed twice. I dove in next to her and buried my face into her neck. My wolf loved to scent her. It would never get old. Her scent just screamed *mine*. Solron had some pretty elaborate tattoos that were different from the tattoos back in my day. Maybe I would get a tattoo, so everyone knew I was hers too.

"Skoll is on the bottom, and Fergus gets the back. But can we all make out first?"

I'd put it wherever she asked me to as long as it made her feel good. I wasn't about all the games Amduscias liked to play in his dungeon. Nothing made me feel better than to make her feel good. It was more than just sex too. Watching how happy she got when she ordered her favorite food put a smile on my face. Her smile just melted my heart. I hoped to see more of that now this was almost over.

Just kissing her was also something that made me happy. I could deal with Fergus being there as we rolled around on the bed, fondling each other and kissing. I loved how she went a little wild when I gave her a few love bites. It wasn't like I was breaking the skin like Roman did.

She got a little rough herself when she rolled me on my back and looked down at me with this fierce expression on her face.

"Do Alpha wolves let fire elementals mount them and ride their cock, or do they always have to be on top?"

I gave her nipple a little pinch.

"This Alpha wolf doesn't mind if a beautiful fire elemental wants to ride his cock."

"Okay, good. I didn't want to hop on your cock unless you were okay with it."

"Well? What are you waiting for? Slide on down it."

It was always unreal when I first entered her, no matter what position we were in. She was tight and wet, and because she was a fire elemental, she was so hot around my cock. She leaned forward on my chest, and all I had to say was that if Fergus was taking her ass, he'd better do this right. His new status of being alive would get cut short if he hurt her.

I realized I didn't need to worry about him. I didn't know how much experience he had in that area, but he'd never hurt her. He demanded lube from Amduscias, who had an entire chest full of toys from his dungeon and took the time to warm her up before he entered her.

She got a million times tighter when she had all of Fergus. Okay, anytime she wanted me to share her like this, I was all up for doing this again. This felt amazing.

"Someone better start fucking me," she said.

Can I tell you how much I loved it when she challenged my wolf? A lot of Alphas were assholes and got furious about it, but not me. I'd never try to put her in her place like some Alphas I'd met. No, when she challenged my wolf, he would always rise to the occasion and show her we could do anything.

I wrapped my arms around her waist and pulled her to my chest. I started thrusting into her. I'd watched Amduscias and Roman do this, but I would do it differently. I would make this last for as long as she could stand it.

Apparently, Fergus felt the same. We were pretty evenly matched, and I could feel his thrusts. We were both going hard but steady. She was squirming and crying out. I would make her scream. I wanted her to remember tonight as much as I hoped she remembered the night I marked her.

I kept my steady pace, but I was having trouble not going hard and fast. The sensation of not being the only one inside her was new, but it was something I wanted to do again. I couldn't unleash my wolf until I knew she was completely satisfied, and I was having trouble controlling him.

I knew how she felt when she came. I knew that little flutter and the cry she made. I grinned when I felt her come around my cock. Fergus felt it too because I heard him chuckle.

"What do you say we leave some for Roman and Amduscias, Skoll?"

"Oh, fine," I grumped.

I wanted to keep going, but I also didn't want to deal with Roman if we wore her out, and he didn't get to play tonight. He'd been promised kinky sex and spankings, and he would be a total ass if he didn't get it. I wouldn't lie. I wanted to let go just as much as I wanted to draw this out.

I crushed her to my chest and just let go. I fucked her hard and fast. My wolf loved every minute of it, and based on the fact that she bit me, she did too. I could feel Fergus had picked up his thrusts as well. We were all out of control. Serafina was clawing and biting. The sting of her nails was just setting me off.

I could feel it coming, but I was thinking about anything else. I wanted her to come again before I did. I would risk Roman's tantrum if she were too tired afterward. I finally let go when I felt her flutter around my cock again.

I hoped she came just as hard as I did. The last time I came that hard was, well, the night I marked her, and mating sex was always super intense. Fergus must have come shortly after I did. We all collapsed in a heap on the bed and just snuggled. I loved this part about sharing her. She never just moved on to the next like we were some line assembly of men in her bed.

It kept us up later, but she always snuggled with us afterward for a while. Snuggling with my mate after I just made her come was just as good as the sex itself. I would just hold her and play with her hair. I loved the way the silken curls felt between my fingers.

I could have gone to sleep just like this. I didn't want to move at all. I knew I would eventually have to get up and let the other men in her life love her.

And I was okay with that because when it was time to sleep, I'd be there right beside her like always.

SERAFINA

There was a lot to be said for being shared with a wolf and a Fae. Fergus and I would have our moment. I just didn't want to do it tonight. He knew that just as much as I did. All of us had been involved in this, so we should all celebrate this victory together. Fergus and I shouldn't just have a few hours after a feast to celebrate his being real. When we did it, it would start at breakfast and end when neither of us could keep our eyes open anymore. It would take way more than a few hours after dinner to celebrate us getting what we had wanted for years.

It was fucking adorable. When I had finally cuddled with Skoll and Fergus enough, I looked over to where Amduscias and Roman were sitting. Roman was sitting in his lap, curled into this little ball. Roman looked like this innocent angel if he didn't open his mouth or get that crazy look in his eyes. He seemed like this huge, naked cherub in

Amduscias's lap. He looked so peaceful with Amduscias playing with his hair.

That didn't last. As soon as he realized I was looking at him, he bolted to his feet like a hungry puppy.

"Is it my turn?"

"Come here, Roman."

I tackled Roman before, but he returned the favor just now. Only Roman would straight-up tackle me like this was the WWE, and I loved that about him. Everyone else treated me like I was this breakable thing to be cherished, but Roman would always play rough with me when I wanted. He'd never hurt me, but he would always play.

Amduscias just stood up and stretched like a cat.

"If you hurt her, I'll punish you, Roman."

"He's fine," I said, running my fingers through his silky blond hair.

Roman sighed and ran his nose from my shoulder to my ear.

"I want to do it like we did before."

I would always give Roman what he wanted. Tonight was about fantasies, and if Roman had one, we would bring it to life. I just laughed.

"Which time, Roman?"

He buried his face in my neck like he was embarrassed after everything, and it was so fucking adorable. I gave Roman a hard squeeze.

"Um, after the dungeon. Can we do that again?"

Amduscias slid into bed and spooned his back.

"We can do anything you want, Roman. All you have to do is ask. I think I speak for Serafina too when I say we both want you happy, and we'll always give you what you want within reason."

Yes, within reason. Just like I couldn't go around killing

people in Hell, I knew there would be some things Roman wanted to that wasn't possible down here, or we would get kicked out. We all had to play by the rules here. I was sure between the Fae and the demons, something would be done with our sentences that we could go topside again.

"Tell us what you want, Roman. It stays in this bedroom. No one will judge," Amduscias said.

"I want you to order me around again. No one has ever done that before, and I liked it. If I mess up, I think I will like it if you punish me."

Well, I'll be damned. Roman was a sub. My psychopathic, serial killing Vampire mate was totally into being dommed by a hot demon, and that was sexy as fuck. I could work with that. There were so many possibilities, but Roman was embarrassed again.

"I want Serafina to play too. I want her to boss me around and punish me. You don't have to if you don't want to. It was just something I was thinking about."

Oh, shit, did Roman just ask me to be his Domme? I'd never done that before, but my interest was piqued. Amduscias had more experience with this than I did. He'd have to teach me so I could do this safely and respectfully with Roman, but I was so fucking down. I could spend extra time with both of them while we figured out how to do this.

"Roman, I would be honored, but if we are going to do this, we will do this right. Which means Amduscias will have to teach me. Is that okay, Amduscias?"

I wanted it, and so did Roman. What about Amduscias? This was his house, and it was his dungeon. Did he even want me to join in that way? I didn't want this to drive a wedge between any of us because we were stepping on his toes. I realized I didn't have to worry when his eyes darkened, and he gave me a smoldering stare.

"Teaching the woman I love how to torture in the bedroom? Nothing would be sexier. Plus, you will need an outlet for your darker side after tomorrow. Bael will not stand for it if people start showing up dead in Hell, even if they were later proved to be criminals. This could be how you channel your darker urges."

Well, fuck. He was right. I would need another hobby after tomorrow. I couldn't exactly take up knitting, and there was a part of me that needed to come out, or I would explode and make a mess. We all had dark sides. Roman was asking me to explore a part of his in a way that would bring him pain and pleasure. Who said my dark side needed to kill? Why couldn't it just be kinky?

"That's actually... perfect. That's a brilliant idea. Thank you, Roman."

"Now, I think Roman had a little fantasy he wanted to play out. Roman, get up and suck my cock. Serafina is going to do whatever the fuck she wants to you, and you are not going to break stride. If she's pleasuring you, you may not come unless she permits you."

"Okay," Roman said.

"No, Roman. You will say *yes, sir* and *no, sir.* When you address Serafina you will say *yes, mistress* and *no, mistress.* Do you understand?"

Roman immediately snapped to attention like he had been doing this his entire life.

"Yes, sir!"

Amduscias rolled on his back and placed his hands behind his head.

"Now, suck my cock."

Roman got on his hands and knees and just went to town. I could have just watched the show and been happy, but I had Roman on all fours, and I could do anything to him within reason. I wasn't going to maim him, but he was right there, and I could just explore his body.

And Roman had a beautiful body. He was pale like all Vampires, but he was also beautifully sculpted. I wanted to touch him and explore his muscles. I ran my hand down his flank all the way to his feet. He broke out into goosebumps. I liked that. I liked him reacting to my touch while he pleasured Amduscias. I started at his shoulders and ran my hands down his back until I got to his ass. He had a nice, perky ass.

I massaged the hard flesh of his ass, then gave him a hard spank. It stung my hand harder than I thought it would. I'd never spanked a guy before because most of the dudes I'd been with would have up and left the room all offended if I had. Roman let out a little grunt and practically waved his reddened ass at me like he wanted more.

My handprint on his ass really stood out on his pale flesh. I had to sit there and admire it for a minute. Roman and Skoll both bit me to claim me. This was my mark on Roman. He was *mine* now. I knew I wasn't supposed to kill anyone down here, but if anyone tried to hurt Roman or come between us they would get burned to a crisp. It was like that for all of them. They were my mates, but they were my family too. I didn't know I needed them, but now that I had them, woe be to anyone who tried to break us up.

I massaged my handprint on Roman's ass for a minute. I knew it stung. It stung my hand too. Once I was sure the sting was gone, I spanked him ten more times, but never in the same spot. I could tell Roman loved every minute of this because he was moaning all over Amduscias's cock and pressing his ass back like he wanted me to keep going. I could get used to this. This could definitely be a replacement for arson and murder.

I didn't know a lot about being a Domme, but I knew about safe sex, and I watched a lot of porn. I knew how Roman wanted this to end, and I didn't want to hurt him. Everyone was so worried about me being hurt and preparing me. I needed to take the same care with Roman if I would do this right.

I hopped off the bed and walked over to Amduscias's treasure chest of sex toys. What to pick? He had an entire sex store in his dungeon, and he brought all the quality stuff up to the bedroom. I'd never done this with a guy before. If I'd even suggested a pinky to one of the guys I'd been with, they probably would have gone off on some homophobic rant, and I'd have to punch them in the face.

Holy shit. He had his sex toys arranged so they were easy to find. All the wands and dildos were together, and the lube and anal toys were all in one place. I picked up that huge, purple dildo he waved at me when he came back from his dungeon. That thing was huge and obscene. Maybe he wouldn't notice if I threw it away or hid it. It looked like a baby arm, and it had glitter in it. If Roman wanted to try it, we could keep it, but this wasn't going anywhere near my girly parts.

Butt toys. I needed butt toys and lube for Roman if we were all going to get nasty later. I liked the ones that vibrated. I thought Roman would too. He even had the butt plugs organized by vibrating and non-vibrating. Amduscias really took his sex toys seriously, and I loved that about him. I also saw several things in this chest I wanted to try later.

I wanted to cheer when I found the perfect butt plug, but I didn't want to distract Roman from his mission. I knew Amduscias would punish him, and I had a feeling Roman would like it. Amduscias was a lot more experienced with this than I was, and his punishment would go a lot further than mine did. Baby steps on the whole BDSM things for now. We didn't have to jump straight into whips and handcuffs.

I climbed back into bed and admired my handiwork on Roman's ass. It was beautiful and red, and some of my handprints stood out. I gave it a gentle rub again. Roman gave me another ass wriggle like he wanted another spanking, but he could get that later.

I squirted lube on his ass and started to massage it in. Roman let out soft little moans. Once everything was nice and slick, I gently slid my finger in. Roman let out a low feral growl and pressed his ass back against me. Oh, he wanted more, did he? My Vampire was so naughty. I'd give him more and then some.

I started fucking him with my finger until he was loosened up. I slipped another finger in and kept working him. Roman moaned when I pulled my fingers out, but I wasn't done with him yet. I rubbed lube into the butt plug and slipped it inside him. Roman straight up growled when I turned it on.

I had more planned for him. I had so much more planned for Roman. I reached around him and started stroking his cock. Roman hissed. He was having so much trouble behaving, but then again, he usually did. He was having trouble not begging me to do what he wanted to his cock while still sucking off Amduscias.

Amduscias finally ended his torture. He patted his shoulder.

"That's enough, Roman. Are you ready for your fantasy to come true?"

"Yes, sir."

"And how did you like your spanking?"

"I wasn't sure about it, but I loved it."

"Then, you should thank your mistress."

Roman turned, and his eyes were glowing red.

"Thank you, Mistress."

"Any time, Roman."

"I liked what you did to my butt too."

Only Roman could make jerking him off after I shoved a vibrating butt plug up his ass sound totally innocent.

"Serafina, why don't you get on your back at the foot of the bed?" Amduscias said.

He didn't have to tell me twice. I had fond memories of this the last time we did this. I hopped on the foot of the bed and spread my legs. I rubbed my aching clit and crooked a finger at Roman. He may have been new to this, but he was catching on fast.

"Do I have permission to fuck you?"

"Yes, you do. Now, get over here."

This was the most restrained I'd ever seen him. Usually, he would have come bounding over to me like a lost puppy. I missed that. I didn't want Roman to change with any of this.

"Roman? Please be yourself. Be goofy and playful."

Amduscias came up behind him and started nibbling on his shoulder.

"I'll expect you to obey our orders, but if I think this is changing you, I will pull the plug on all of it."

Roman's entire body relaxed.

"Oh, thank God. I thought I was supposed to be acting a certain way. Here I come, Serafina!"

Roman went running and jumped on top of me. He started nuzzling my neck with his nose like he always did. I had to permit him now, didn't I? This was so weird and new. I grabbed his face and made him look at me.

"You have my permission to bite me when you want, but

this only goes in the bedroom. If you need to feed, you can always bite me."

"Thank you, mistress."

I would have to get used to this whole mistress thing, but I kind of dug it. I'd have to not let it go to my head. I mean, a hot Vampire calling me *mistress* and doing my bidding? I could get off on that.

"Make love to me, Roman. Bite me when you are ready."

Roman let out a little snarl. Feral Roman was back as he slid into me. He immediately calmed when Amduscias placed a hand on his back.

"Do you want to go this alone, or do you want me too?"

Roman craned his head over his shoulder and gave Amduscias a cheeky wink.

"Of course I want you too. Get over here, you big sexy demon."

"That mouth, Roman," Amduscias said, stroking his back.

Roman pressed into me even deeper when Amduscias slid into him. That was what I loved so much about this. It was like I got more of Roman with Amduscias's additional weight. They both started moving. Roman was a little more restrained this time, but he was still wild. Roman fucked like a jackhammer, but sometimes, a girl needed a jackhammer in the bedroom if the guy knew how to do it right.

And Roman knew how to do it perfectly.

I arched my back and raked my nails down his arms. There was one thing I could say about fucking Roman. It was always passionate and fucking *hot*. Especially with Amduscias behind him fucking his ass. Every time Roman would thrust into me, Amduscias would thrust into him, and it was like this double-tap. We were sharing Roman, but it was like making love to both of them at the same time.

It never took long with Roman. With the pace he kept, I'd have to be numb from the waist down not to have an orgasm screaming at me shortly after he got started. When it hit, it was so intense, and I bit him this time. Roman's red eyes met mine.

"Yes, bite me, my love."

"Only if you bite me too," I gasped.

Roman buried his face in my neck, but he didn't bite me. When he bit me, I would come again. I already knew that. How hard it depended on how much he worked me up again.

And worked me up he did. Between Amduscias and Roman, I think we all went a little feral. Roman wasn't the only one snarling and hissing. All three of us were. Amduscias gave Roman's ass a hard spanking.

"You have permission now."

Was that what Roman was waiting for? I'd forgotten all about that. I forgot all about thinking about it, too, when Roman buried his fangs in my neck. My nails drew blood as they raked down his back. I nearly bucked hard enough to make both of them fly across the room. Pleasure surged through me, and all I could do was claw Roman and ride it out.

It never seemed to end. My body was shaking, and every time I thought it was over, another wave of pleasure would hit me. When it was finally over, we pulled ourselves to the top of the bed and collapsed.

Fergus and Skoll joined us. Skoll always held me when we slept, and Amduscias and Roman took turns. Skoll knew he would have to share now that Fergus was real, but he also knew how much Fergus being real meant to me. He let Fergus climb in first with no argument.

Fergus pulled me to his chest while Amduscias spooned my back.

"Are you happy, my Ena?" Fergus asked.

"Yeah, I am. But we are getting our moment when this is over. And it will be an all-day thing. Start planning what you want to do."

"I want to try a cheeseburger. They don't have them in the Fae realm, and I know you like them. I didn't need to eat when I was a guardian."

Okay, then it was settled. My day with Fergus would involve eating and fucking.

SERAFINA

I don't think I'd ever slept that well in my entire life. I felt safe and whole, and I knew exactly why. I had them all there with me now. Fergus was real now, and I slept in his arms. We were all snuggled into Amduscias's enormous bed, and I was finally home. I didn't care that Skoll snored, or Roman threatened to kill people in his sleep. When that happened, I just settled and went right back to sleep. If it had been anyone else, I would have high-tailed it out of the bed so fast. With Skoll and Roman, I just found it fucking adorable. I found myself smiling every time Roman would get a little twitch and threaten to rip some-one's head off in his sleep.

I stretched when I woke up. I pretty much never wanted to leave this bed. My head was resting on Fergus's chest, and Amduscias was spooning my back with his face buried in my neck. A girl could get used to this. I didn't even want to get out of bed to go murder a bunch of witches, and I was always up for killing some bad guys. What the fuck was wrong with me?

As much as I didn't want to move, every single man in my bed jumped up as soon as my stomach growled. Of course, my stomach would betray me. I'd gone hungry plenty of times on the street and learned to ignore it. It didn't bother me. But my men? Now that they knew I spent a lot of time hungry growing up, if they so much as suspected I was hungry, they would throw food at me until I ate. Not that there was anything wrong with four passionate guys feeding you. That was sexy as fuck.

"What do you want for breakfast?" Amduscias asked.

What *did* I want to eat? I had so many options now. After I got a job and an apartment, breakfast was coffee and what I could put in the toaster. I had a feeling Amduscias and his chef would take offense at Pop-Tarts. Hell, I got offended by Pop-Tarts, but I ate them anyway because they were quick and cheap. I ate them because I liked to sleep in more than I hated Pop-Tarts.

"Um, I've got no idea. I always ate shitty, processed food for breakfast. The oatmeal at the convent was just as bad as the oatmeal at Scorchwood. Can you pick something?"

"Ah. Then we will have a house specialty. Cashew and Saffron Donuts, Chestnut Infused Venison, and I'll have him make some of his praline bonbons. Sound good?"

Did that sound good? It seemed a million times better than shitty oatmeal or Pop-Tarts. My bed was now empty, and I was hungry. Starving actually, but then again, I was always hungry.

"I'm going to get a gigantic ass living here."

"Highly doubtful, my Ena. You've always been able to eat whatever you wanted, and even then, you've always been too skinny."

I swatted his arm.

"Are you saying you don't like my body?"

"I'm saying if Amduscias is going to be spanking you too, I'd like a little more padding there. You're perfect as you are."

"I don't want to step on any toes, but we have a mission to take down those witches. Eiltan, Charley, and Finn all want to come. We should invite them to breakfast so we can all talk strategy before we leave."

"Of course. I'm not going to get upset if you invite him. He proved he wasn't a total shit in the end. He wasn't the one who framed me and experimented on me anyway. He's already told me if he knew they had framed me, he would have gotten me out of there, and he had his own people looking into my conviction."

I pulled Skoll, Roman, and Fergus back to bed while Amduscias got busy on his phone making calls. You can't blame a bitch for wanting more snuggles. I didn't snuggle with pretty much any of the guys I got up with topside, but I could already tell you all my men snuggled better than any man in any realm.

Amduscias hung his phone up and flung himself in bed with us.

"If we didn't have shit to do, I would so say breakfast in bed. I never ate in bed before Serafina introduced me to takeout and movies."

"I want to watch the other movies with the little green man," Roman said.

Roman had really latched onto Yoda. He thought the way Yoda talked was hilarious. When Roman wasn't saying totally Roman things or threatening to kill someone, he liked to pretend to speak like Yoda. I may utterly lose my shit if he started threatening to kill people *while* talking like

Yoda. Seriously, there would be no way for me to keep a straight face.

"There are three prequels, and they've made a few movies after, but they don't have the same characters."

"But is the little green man in it?"

I sighed. I would have to show them those prequels, and I swear, if Roman latched onto Jar Jar Binks and started talking like him, I may scream. Then again, if we could get it down here, Roman would lose his shit over Baby Yoda.

"I liked the movies too, Serafina. I wouldn't mind watching the other movies," Skoll said.

"It's a date then. After we murder all the witches, we can have a feast in bed and have a *Star Wars* marathon."

This was my new life, and I loved every minute of it— sex, snuggles, and teaching these guys about the modern world. I wanted more of it. As much as I loved being Elemental Batwoman, maybe it was good that she had to retire. I'd found an outlet for that that didn't hurt anyone.

That didn't mean I wasn't looking forward to killing those witches. It was their fault I ended up in Scorchwood and Rathmore experimented on me. All so they could get me pregnant and get more power. They hadn't even perfected their technique yet. Skinner had stolen power, but she couldn't use it. I wasn't a scientist, and I wasn't some power-hungry witch, but if I were, I would have tried to get my own shit straight before I upped my experiments on other people. I would have figured out how to unlock my stolen power before I raised my framing game.

There was a knock on the door. Alozan came in. I liked her. She never reacted or judged when she came in, and we were all in bed in various states of undress. And we were all totally ass naked right now.

"Breakfast will be ready in ten minutes. I've alerted your

guests. The Fae will be portalling in, and the witches borrowed a car. They are already on their way."

"Thank you, Alozan," Amduscias said.

We all started getting dressed, and I was still amazed at the clothes down here. There were fancy clothes for going out, comfortable clothes for lounging around the house, and I even found the perfect murder clothes for when we went to kill the witches. I'd managed to perfect my murder outfits when I was topside, but the ones in Hell were even better.

We arrived downstairs just as Charley and Finn came in. Eiltan portalled in shortly after. I was wondering about that. My father could open portals because he was Fae. Fergus hadn't taught me that, but could I do it too?

"Can I open portals like that?"

"I think so," Fergus said. "I never taught you because I didn't want you to know you were more Fae than the other elementals."

"I'm almost certain you can. I can teach you if you like. You probably have a lot more gifts you haven't tapped into yet. Fergus wouldn't have been able to teach you and keep you safe. If I had known about you, I would have taught you once I knew you could keep it a secret."

I knew why I hadn't been taught all my Fae powers, but it was pretty fucking cool I would learn. Fergus and my father could teach me together. I could get to know my father on neutral territory. We wouldn't be talking about our feelings or the past. He would teach me about my heritage without all the past hurt. I couldn't be mad at him for not being there for me growing up when he didn't know my mother ran away to a convent. I was sure those evil nuns made it super hard to find her since they thought she was having some demonic pregnancy.

"I'd like that, but won't you be busy in the Fae realm?"

I guess maybe I was still looking for reasons to be mad at him. He had no way of knowing my mother was pregnant in a convent, but I spent decades pretty furious at him. It was almost like it was a part of me. I needed to let go of that shit. I took a massive leap with Skoll, Roman, and Amduscias and look where that got me. I was happy, and I had a home.

"I messed up and missed a lot of your life, Serafina. I don't intend to make that mistake again if you let me be a part of your life."

That was so the right thing to say. And I wanted that. The whole time I was in prison and hated him, I still wanted him to come to me and say that. Now that I heard it, it was like some of my broken pieces were starting to heal.

"I'd like that a lot."

"I'd like to see you in action with these witches. You'd make quite the Fae queen if you wanted the title. I think you've done more in a few weeks than my family has in a few generations."

"And now I'd just like a nice, boring life where I'm not getting framed and stopping naughty royalty."

Eiltan looked at all my men with this look on my face.

"I hope you all realize she's a princess back in the Fae realm and treat her as such."

I groaned. Did he just go all dad on me and have a dad talk with my men? I hoped some sex talk wasn't forthcoming. I knew he didn't have a chance to threaten my boyfriends when I was younger, but I wasn't a teenager anymore.

Amduscias just lifted my hand to his mouth and kissed my knuckle.

"She's still royalty here in Hell. Eventually, she will be a Duchess."

We all filed into Amduscias's dining hall. I was still

processing eventually becoming a Duchess of Hell. That was just all kinds of fucked up. Who in their right mind wanted me in charge of anything? I couldn't even keep a houseplant alive. Now, both the Fae and the demons were ready to put a crown on my head and call me royalty. I would fuck that up somehow, even if I didn't end up killing someone.

"Bael gave me intel on these witches while we were working in the lab for the remedy on the Fae. A few shadow demons have been spying on them. They are in a castle in a remote area of Romania, but the castle is heavily fortified and warded. They will know when we arrive on their territory, and they've laid magical traps all over the property."

Charley just tipped her juice in a salute.

"That's why you bring two witches with you. Between the two of us, we can disarm them. You just need to kill them before they start flinging curses."

My father just gave this evil grin.

"Between my daughter, Fergus, and myself, we've got enough firepower to torch the entire castle."

Was my father offering to murder some witches with me? That was so sweet. This was the kind of father-daughter bonding I could get behind. A family that murders together stay together, right?

"Unless you don't want me to?" he asked. "That coven was responsible for the mess in Scorchwood, and they hurt you. I want revenge just as much as you do."

"Are you kidding? It's pretty cool that you will burn some evil witches with me."

"Bael said this is the last time in Hell, right? I can bring you in on the Fae justice system if you really like punishing the wicked. We don't have a lot of crime, but people do still act up."

"No, I think it's time to put this part of my life behind me. It was good while it lasted, but I think I've found something to replace it."

"I'm glad. A forest surrounds the castle. Bael thinks it would be best to portal in near the front, but outside of the range of the traps. A witch could clear a path from a distance, giving us a way to get close and start a fire."

"When can we leave?" I asked.

"As soon as you finish your breakfast, young lady," Eiltan said.

I couldn't decide if it was fucking adorable he was trying to dad me right before we went to murder people, or I wanted to punch him in the face for trying to tell me what to do.

SERAFINA

pparently, we weren't going evil witch-hunting right off. Three people in our hunting party could open a portal to Romania and get us there, but they all wanted me to do it. I was good at killing people and setting shit on fire, but how did they know I would not open a portal in the middle of the ocean, and we would all drown. I had questions. They were all working against me too. No one had my back that one of the Fae or a demon should open this portal, and they could teach me afterward.

"You can do this, my Ena. You tapped into your Fae magic to open that secret door in Scorchwood. Don't you want to learn more about your gifts?"

Yeah, I did, but not in front of everyone. I thought these would be private lessons with Eiltan and Fergus. I was being a fucking baby. No one would judge me if I fucked up, and Fergus had always been an excellent teacher. I would not open a portal to the top of the Statue of Liberty with him teaching me. It was like everything else Fergus tried to teach me. I needed to concentrate and get my shit together.

I shook out my hands and squared my shoulders.

"Okay, let's do this. How do I open a portal?"

"It starts in your gut," Eiltan said.

"He's right," Fergus said. "Your magic is based on fire, and you already know how to use it. Let it pool in your belly, but don't let it out to set anything on fire. Tell the fire to do your bidding and become pure magic. You'll feel it when it changes. It will go from being warm to cool. It's then you'll be able to do things with it that don't hurt anything. Imagine the witches. Tell the magic you feel that you want to go to the witch and send it out. The portal will open, and you'll be right where you want to be."

Eiltan was nodding.

"My lessons on portalling were much harsher, but that's how you do it. In time, it will become second nature, and you can open the portal in an instant."

This would not happen unless I tried, and I always tried everything at least once, even if it was stupid and got me in trouble. Amduscias and Eiltan made portalling look so easy, but I felt like I had this big, ugly vein popping out in my forehead that would burst and cause a mess.

This was just like everything else. I'd have to practice. Neither Fergus nor Eiltan knew if this was something a halfling could do, but I wasn't stopping until I knew for sure it wasn't. If the door to the Fae realm was being reopened, there would possibly be a lot more halflings in the world, and I was now their ambassador. I'd never been important anywhere I went before, and I didn't really want to be now, but better me be a guinea pig than a bunch of halflings come into this world not knowing what they could and couldn't do. I had a prince and a guardian to teach me. I'm sure Eiltan had all the best tutors growing up, and Fergus was a guardian for a reason.

How did you tell fire to behave and turn itself into magic? That was the one thing about my element. Sure, I could unleash it and control it to a point, but if you let your control slip for even just a moment, the fire would become bigger than you and burn anything that got in its way.

That was the key. How did I control the flames when they wanted to rage out of control? It was always sheer will and a firm command. This was *my* fire, and it had to do what I said. I always spoke sweet words to my fire when I was giving it commands. I thought it just behaved better that way.

"Come on, baby. You know you want to become magic for mama. Don't let me down."

I felt it! I felt the temperature drop like someone just poured ice water inside me. My fire was a part of me, and it was just like me. You had to sweet talk both us to get us to do anything.

"Let's go kill some witches, baby. I'll let you burn the entire place to the ground if you just get us there."

Like with me, bribery also helped. I laughed and pumped my fist as a beautiful portal opened up. I grabbed the nearest person and hugged them. Then shit just got all awkward when I realized it was Eiltan and not Fergus. Why did it always have to be uncomfortable? I was deciding right now, no more awkwardness. We put down a rebellion and cured the Fae together. Who said I couldn't hug him without it being weird?

I threw my arms back around his neck and squeezed him.

"Ha! Did you see that shit? I made a portal!"

I got hugs from all my men and smiles from Charley and Finn. My father just smiled at me.

"I knew you could do it. I can't wait to teach you all of your gifts."

"What all can I do?"

"You have the gift of tongues. You can understand any language out there once you learn how to use it. It's quite useful when you are making deals. Fae are weakened by iron. It can kill us, but your human blood cuts down on that drastically. I think, at most, you might be a little uncomfortable touching it, but I would avoid getting any into your system. We don't do it often, but the Fae can shape shift in the sense that we can change our size and get smaller. It helped for spying during wars. Not much of that goes on anymore."

"Badass," I said.

Fergus snapped me back to reality.

"We should get through that portal before it closes, my Ena."

Now was the moment of truth. When we stepped through that portal, were we going to be outside a castle in Romania or smack dab in the middle of the ocean surrounded by sharks?

SERAFINA

I'd never been to Romania before. I'd never even been outside of the US. When I stepped through the portal, I saw a castle and an unfamiliar landscape. Did I do it? Did I make a portal to another country? This opened up so many possibilities. If I knew they weren't going to arrest us again topside, there were so many places I could visit on vacation now. I was picturing my guys half-naked on a beach in Greece while we all rubbed suntan lotion on each other and drank fruity drinks.

I felt bodies crowd around with me. My father put his hand on my shoulder, but I didn't shrug it off. I found it didn't bother me as much.

"This is it. They must have suspected I had something to do with Skinner's disappearance because there is iron all over the place. I can't get close."

"Neither can I. It's uncomfortable even being out here," Fergus said.

Roman and Skoll came up to stand beside us.

"Iron doesn't bother us. If Charley and Finn can take any nasty magic down, we can remove any iron we see and move it away. I don't want to risk it hurting Serafina too," Skoll said.

I couldn't sense iron like Eiltan and Fergus could, but there was something about that castle that made me not want to go near it. Good thing we had a team with us. Why hadn't I ever murdered people using teamwork before? Oh, yeah. The more people involved, the more likely I was to get caught. Someone would always get caught and blab on the rest of the group to get a lighter sentence. I didn't mind snitches when they brought me a bad guy to kill, but I didn't want one ratting on me.

Charley and Finn stepped forward, cracking their knuckles.

"They've got some pretty nasty traps on the property. Nothing we can't undo, but once their wards are down, they will feel it and know we are here. If someone will be going in and removing iron, best let Roman do it because he can move too fast for them to see. If they can't see him, they have less of a chance of hitting him with anything."

Roman just shrugged.

"The iron isn't going to be buried, is it?"

Fergus grinned.

"If they were smart, they would have buried it, but they didn't. They have iron totems around the property."

"And some of their protection spells are in those totems, so hold your horses, Roman. Just because iron doesn't affect you don't mean the spells on them won't."

"Can you break all those spells from here? I don't want to put anyone in danger," I said.

Finn pulled some sort of device out of his rucksack and set it on the ground.

"I told you all I enjoyed working with my hands, right? This is a device of my own invention. It's helpful when going up against a coven when you don't have a clear shot. It's kind of like a magical EMT. All I have to do is press this button, and it will disable any magic around the property."

That sounded great and all, but I still had questions.

"What about us? Technically, we are all magical creatures. Is it going to neuter us, so we have to fight them with fucking rocks? None of us have guns."

"Yes, but I found a solution to that before I ever used this device. Charley?"

Charley brought a rucksack too. She started pulling out these coins on leather straps and handing them out. I had no idea what it was, but I slipped it over my neck. If a warlock told you they were about to set off a magic bomb and handed you a coin, you put it on. I wasn't stupid.

"It was a lot of trial and error, but I found a spell to put on these coins that are immune to the EMT. Now, when I set this off, it will disable the wards, and anything magical within a fifty-mile radius will lose their powers for about six hours unless they have one of these coins. Whatever you do, make sure you have this coin on at all times. It's not really an EMT. It's a long-lasting spell. If you take the coin off or someone takes it off, you might as well be human. Get it?"

I got it loud and clear, and so did everyone else. We hadn't known Finn long, but we knew he was an assassin with toys and a powerful warlock. There was no telling what was in that fucking rucksack, but if he started handing out dead toads and said they protected us from something in there, we'd happily wear them.

Once we all had our necklaces on, Finn placed his

device on the ground and pressed a button. He ran back to us, and at first, I wasn't sure what was supposed to happen. When it finally went off, boy, did I find out. A blinding white light went off, and even with the coin around my neck, I turned around and barfed everywhere. I hadn't felt that sick since college and an incident with watermelon vodka.

I think we all ended up puking, even Finn. He wiped his mouth and gave us this apologetic look.

"That was the one thing I couldn't get rid of with these coins. It'll go away in about five minutes, and then we can make our move."

"Speak for yourself. I just vomited blood," Roman moaned.

Amduscias and I both snapped to attention. I knew the witches and warlocks would be without power, but I didn't want Roman going in there to remove all the iron totems so we could get close. What if they hired a shifter for some old-fashioned booby traps around the property? Roman needed to be as fast as possible, and for that, he needed blood. He took some from both Amduscias and me before he disappeared into a blur to remove everything.

Eiltan just chuckled. He hadn't said a single thing about me having several men in my life until now. I didn't know how he felt about it.

"Fate did well pairing you with him. I like the way he looks at you, and his speed is quite handy. He's already gotten most of the totems. Can you feel it?"

"Yeah, actually, I do. There was something about the place that made me not want to come close. I didn't know if it was the magic or the iron, but it's starting to feel safer to get close. I still can't tell where the totems are like you can."

"They are gone now, my Ena. Roman got all of them."

"Then, where the fuck is Roman? He should be back by now."

I didn't like this. I didn't want Roman going off by himself to take care of something when we were here as a team. If he didn't come back soon, I was going in and burning anything that got in my way.

Roman didn't make me worry long. He skidded to a stop in front of me. I flung myself in his arms and squeezed him.

"Any trouble?"

"I tried to get a closer look on my last trip. They are all congregated by an open window on the second floor. That's where I sensed all the heartbeats. They are trying not to be seen while looking out the window to figure out why they don't have magic anymore."

Roman was safe. Fergus and Eiltan would be safe if we got close. The witches were now powerless. What could go wrong?

SERAFINA

Since I had a fire dragon and liked to kill people, I used to have this long-standing fantasy about storming a castle and taking out the bad guys like some hero in the books I liked to read once I could afford them. Shut up. You know if you had a dragon, you'd be thinking that too. It looked like my fantasy was about to come to life—what a way to retire Elemental Batwoman.

Okay, so we didn't exactly storm the castle. We snuck up quietly and carefully just in case because Finn said we should still expect anything. We gathered behind some trees just outside the window Roman found. Without their magic, it was hard to sense them. I could always sense supernatural creatures, but without a magical signature to home in on, it was a lot more complicated.

Finn didn't have that trouble. He was aiming his big fucking gun right at the window.

"They are in there, but I don't have a shot."

I was curious. How did he sense them, but I couldn't?

"How do you know?"

"My scope picks up heat signatures. Not everything has to be done by magic, you know."

Well, I was doing this by magic. I was burning those bitches alive. I stuck my head out from behind the tree and flicked my wrist so the curtains caught on fire. I heard a loud crack of gunfire. It wasn't Finn, or my ears would have been ringing. Fergus yanked me back and slammed me into the tree. He ripped my shirt open.

"Are you okay?" he yelled.

"Yeah, why?"

"You're hit, my Ena. And based on the wound, they used iron bullets."

I couldn't feel anything. I didn't know someone had shot me. My adrenaline was pumping too hard, and I was feeling no pain. I was feeling some pretty intense rage, though. Those bitches *shot* me. I'd never been shot before, but I already knew this would eventually hurt when my blood stopped pumping, and who knew what an iron bullet would do to me when I wasn't pure Fae?

"Nobody shoots me and lives," I growled.

Eiltan was furious.

"They just shot Fae royalty, and I won't stand for that. Fergus, have you taught her to channel?"

"We need to get her out of here," Fergus argued.

"No, those assholes are dying right now. You can take me back to Hell after I've killed them."

"Then, grab my hand, Serafina," Eiltan said.

Eiltan held out his hand, and Fergus held out his. I got the feeling this wasn't some hippy moral support thing because I'd just been shot, so I grabbed their hands and squeezed. Eiltan and Fergus linked hands, and Eiltan's eyes were boring into me.

"We are burning those witches, and then you are leaving immediately for medical treatment. We can't leave that bullet in too long, or you'll get iron poisoning. You have a little longer than Fergus, or I would because you are not full Fae, and the bullet hit your shoulder."

"She's still bleeding," Fergus argued.

"They die now, Fergus. Serafina, call to your fire and let it mingle with mine and Fergus's. Let it rage as hot as you can, but don't release it."

I'd never done this before, but I was able to call more fire and even hotter than usual when I was holding hands with Fergus and Eiltan. This was pretty fucking cool, but I had no idea where Eiltan was going with this. I usually had to see something to set it on fire, and I didn't want Fergus and Eiltan sticking their heads out from around this tree if they were shooting Fae kryptonite.

"Now, on three, we need to imagine all the fire we are holding going to that room the witches and warlocks are in. Are you ready?"

When he said three, I did what he asked and holy shit—the second floor where the window was exploded into flame. I'd burned plenty of buildings and people but never had that result before. It always took time for the fire to build. When I craned my head around the tree, the roof was already on fire.

No one could have survived that fire, and it started in a way they couldn't have put it out. Everyone in there was dead. We did it, but I was beginning to get dizzy.

I started laughing.

"I finally got my revenge for those assholes sending me to Scorchwood and experimenting on me."

That was the last thing I said because I passed out after that.

FERGUS

I was furious at Eiltan. He should have had my back about Serafina getting treatment for that bullet. He knew just as well as I did that iron poisoning was no joke. Neither of us knew how it would affect a halfling, but I'd spent her entire life trying to keep as much iron out of her life as possible. That was my error. If I'd made a bigger deal about it, she would have known this was serious and left before we took out those witches. I would have gone back myself and killed them for shooting her.

Serafina was passed out in Doctor Bogthon's clinic, and I didn't think he should be treating her. There were no Fae in Hell. I didn't think elementals had the same reaction to iron. Did he even know how to handle this? Serafina needed to be treated by a Fae doctor.

He wouldn't even let any of us in the room, and he warned me not to go in there as my invisible form to spy either because I might startle him. The only reason I wasn't in there looking over his shoulder was that I didn't want to do that. Instead, I was picking fights with Eiltan.

"She needs to be back with the Fae getting this treated. You should have made her leave!"

Eiltan just shrugged.

"Could you have made her leave? She's known you longer than she's known me. Could you have gotten her to leave before they were all dead? Can you say with a straight face that you didn't want them dead for shooting her? If we left, they would have moved, and we might have lost them for good. They would have put up better protection, and people could have died this time."

"She might be in there dying now!" I yelled.

"She won't, Fergus. Once the bullet is out, she will just need chelation therapy."

I just sat there and grumped. I already knew he was right about her refusing to leave until the witches were dead. She would have taken it as an affront to her person that one of them shot her. If they had just shot *at* her and not hit her, I would have resumed my dragon form in an instant and burned that entire castle down. It was different when I knew the bullet struck her, then I saw the black strands spreading from the wound and realized it was an iron bullet.

I was going crazy, and I needed to burn something or someone. The witches were already dead, and I already knew Bael would be mad if I killed someone here. I wouldn't mind beating the crap out of Eiltan for not helping me make her leave, but I already knew how that would go down. It would be the one thing we fought over, and I'd end up coming between them. Eiltan was on her side, and I wasn't. That would be all she saw if I beat her father up.

Skoll, Amduscias, and Roman came to sit next to me.

"I don't know a thing about iron poisoning. What does it

mean for her? She wasn't acting like anything was wrong until she passed out," Skoll said.

I didn't feel weird sharing Fae secrets with them. I knew they would never use it against my people, and if they knew this, they could help me keep Serafina safe.

"Iron weakens Fae. If you keep us in iron chains, we can barely move. If it gets into the bloodstream, it becomes fatal. It's supposed to be a long, painful death that way. I've got no idea how that affects Serafina since she's half Fae, but her wound reacted the same as I've seen for iron poisoning. It's considered a dirty way to kill someone back where I come from. There's no iron in the Fae realm. Only the truly dishonorable risk trying to sneak some in to give someone iron poisoning. It could kill them too."

Roman chewed on his bottom lip.

"If there's no iron in the Fae realm, then isn't there no treatment? Isn't the best place for her here in Hell?"

Well, I'll be damned. Sometimes, that crazy Vampire said the damnedest things that made sense. As far as I knew, there *wasn't* a remedy in the Fae realm, but I'd learned from living topside with Serafina that humans could get iron poisoning too from vitamins and supplements. I'd researched that because I didn't want Serafina near any iron.

If humans could treat iron poisoning, it made sense Hell could too. And Hell had a remedy tailored for supernatural beings. I clapped Roman on the back.

"Thanks. That actually makes me feel better."

Eiltan was still pacing, but he didn't look as worried as I felt.

"The Fae got our remedy for iron poisoning from human research. It does work. We've used it on Fae who were exposed when they came topside for business. We learned the hard way not to take certain vitamins topside. We thought they might help us back in the Fae realm, but the ones with iron made us sick. Instead, we researched and formulated our own. Serafina is in capable hands."

I stood and balled my fists. I was having trouble not punching Eiltan. Both of his eyes were already nearly swollen shut, and it looked like Doctor Bogthon had reset his nose where Serafina broke it. I wanted to break it again and knock out a few teeth.

"I don't care if you knew the treatment would work. She had just been shot. That should have been your priority, not revenge on those witches."

"My priority *was* getting her out of there. We both know she would not leave until they were dead. It would have been quicker to channel our fire and kill them than it would have been to talk her into leaving. If we had stayed there any longer trying to get her to leave, we might have found out they had weapons that could have killed us both. Would you like your face to look like mine because you portalled her home without her consent? She beat the shit out of Zepar and me for doing that."

"You both had it coming," I pouted, sitting down.

I knew everything he said was right, but I also felt so fucking helpless right now. I should have been in there with her. Since I had a flesh and blood body now, I couldn't see things through her eyes anymore. I couldn't visit her dreams unless I was asleep, and I was way too keyed up to sleep right now. I wanted to punch something, and Eiltan was right there looking very punchable.

I knew I should have been blaming that fucking coven. They were the ones who framed her and experimented on her. One of them pulled the trigger and shot her. They were all burned to a crisp, and I couldn't kill them a second time, so I was blaming Eiltan. I knew it wasn't rational, and I'd eventually have to apologize to him, but I couldn't help what I was feeling right now. I was her guardian! She wasn't supposed to be getting shot when she was with me.

I was about to just start breaking things in the room when Doctor Bogthon finally came out. We all jumped to our feet and crowded around him. The first words out of his mouth better be that she was just fine and resting. Everyone else felt the same way as I did. I was just the only one throwing a tantrum like a baby Fae.

"The bullet didn't hit anything major, and it was a clean wound. I was able to get it out, and I've got her on an IV to help with the iron poisoning. There's a water demon sitting with her healing the wound now."

"Can we see her?" we all said at once.

Doctor Bogthon must deal with a lot of eager men who were willing to kill someone if their mate got hurt because he knew just how to deal with us.

"I'd let you in there right now, even though she is sleeping, but water demons need peace and quiet to heal. You're all quite agitated right now and for a good reason. If you leave her alone with Serafina for another hour, when she wakes up, the wound will be healed, and she'll only have a slight amount of soreness. Can you do that for me?"

I could put a lid on my rage and stop acting like a teenager for an hour if it meant she wouldn't hurt when she woke up.

But only an hour. After an hour, I was kicking that door down.

SKOLL

My wolf and I were going just as crazy as Fergus was acting, but if I didn't sit here and concentrate on my breathing, I would shift and kill someone. I didn't blame Eiltan like he was doing. I think Fergus knew deep down doing what Eiltan did was the only way she would leave. If there were armed witches and warlocks in that window with a gun like Finn's, if anyone had opened a portal and tried to throw her through it to make her leave, she could have gotten hit again, or more of us could have gotten shot. Someone could have died. Someone other than those fucking witches and warlocks.

I spent hundreds of years in Scorchwood with no outside stimulation, but that hour in the waiting room while the water demon healed her felt way longer than my years in jail. I was trying so hard not to wolf out in the middle of this waiting room.

There was so much I didn't understand. Fergus and

Eiltan were talking about iron poisoning and IVs. I had no idea what any of that meant. I didn't understand the world around me anymore, and it was hitting me so hard right now because I couldn't understand what was being done to treat my mate.

I suppose all I really needed to know was that she would be okay, and, in an hour, it would be like no one shot her, but still, when was anything going to make sense? Why did they even make guns like the one Finn carried, and if iron weakness was such a Fae secret, how did the witches and warlocks know about it to get iron bullets made?

I liked Doctor Bogthon. I liked him when he gave me an exam because he answered all my stupid questions, and the treatments he recommended were strengthening me. I trusted him to help Serafina, and he did. I just needed to see her with my own two eyes and touch her.

Doctor Bogthon came out as soon as our hour was up.

"You can go in now. She's awake. I will need to ask her a few questions. Please let me finish, and then you can talk to her."

We all scrambled to our feet and went running. She was sitting up in bed like she was waiting for us. They had changed her clothing, and she was wearing some strange shift. Her arm was wrapped in some device like it was still injured.

"I thought you said she was healed?" I growled. "Why does she have that thing on her arm?"

"It's just a sling. She will have a limited range of motion for a few days. Do you mind?"

Serafina didn't let him talk either.

"What the fuck just happened? I woke up, and a woman was standing over me, and my arm was cold. And why the fuck do I have to pee so badly?"

"Water demons have healing power. She was healing your wound. You'll have to keep that sling on for a few days, but your pain should be minimal. You'll have to stay here and finish the chelation treatment for iron poisoning. One of the side effects is frequent urination. How are you feeling right now? Any pain or nausea? How is your stomach?"

"I'm pissed off. One of those witches fucking *shot* me, and I can only kill someone once."

"Yes, aside from being angry, how do you feel physically? Any pain?"

"No, the water demon took care of that. Can I thank her later? Aside from being pissed and having to pee, I'm just fine. When can I go home?"

"You got shot with an iron bullet, Serafina. You can't go home right away. You aren't Superwoman."

"No, I'm Elemental Batwoman," she pouted.

"I'm sorry?" he said.

"Nothing. Can I pee?"

We all jumped up to help her, but my wolf had finally calmed down. She was back to being prickly and sassy, just the way I liked her. She didn't seem like she was in pain either. I could feel it through our mate bond now that she was awake. Her shoulder was a dull ache like mine was sometimes after an intense workout.

I still needed to touch her. My wolf needed to scent her and make sure she wasn't sick. I didn't know the first thing about iron poisoning or what the fuck chelation therapy was, but I trusted my nose, and it would tell me if she was sick.

She wasn't limping when she came out of the bathroom, but she had a demon, a Fae, and a Vampire fussing over her. I gave her space because I knew she hated it when people made a big deal over her. She was still getting used to letting people take care of her.

I pounced as soon as she got back into bed. She was giggling as I sniffed her from head to toe. She grabbed me when I got to her head and gave me a passionate kiss.

"What does your wolf say? Do I stink?"

I nuzzled her neck.

"You smell delicious. Whatever Doctor Bogthon did to you, you don't smell as sick as you did after you got shot."

"I agree," Roman said, taking her other hand.

"You should never have been shot under my watch, my Ena," Fergus said.

"Stop that, Fergus. How were we to know the witches had guns? Aside from Finn, most witches and warlocks don't use them."

"Still, I should have been prepared for anything."

"Don't do that, Fergus. I was the one that stuck my head out from behind the tree to start the fire. This isn't your fault. Besides, once this IV finishes, I'll be good as new. Right, doctor?"

"She's right. And look on the bright side. It will please Bael to know those witches are dead. He sent a message earlier. He demanded top treatment for Serafina. The only reason he hasn't come was that he knew she would pull through, and he's given Warden Skinner another round of torture to see if she's withholding any information."

"She fears me. Could I get out of here sooner if I could get more information out of her? I can't kill her coven a second time, but I wouldn't mind taking out on her the fact that those assholes shot me."

"No!" we all yelled at the same time.

She could have her funsies on Warden Skinner *after* she completed her treatment.

SERAFINA

So, we stopped a hostile takeover of Hell, and some witches fucking *shot* me. Bael was being a total spoilsport and wouldn't let me anywhere near Warden Skinner. He thought I would maim her to the point she got dead. Honestly, I probably would, so I let it drop.

I'd done my treatment and peed a lot. I was released from the hospital, and now it was time to go to the Fae realm with my father. I was stressing about it. Ior had started bringing the treatments back and spreading the word that I helped to do it. Eiltan said people wanted to meet me, but I had my doubts.

"What are they going to say when we get there, and they see what I did to your face? You're a prince for fuck's sake!"

Eiltan just laughed.

"They'll say you're a true Sunshadow, my dear. Now, are you ready?"

I so wasn't. We were supposed to go after breakfast, and I

so wasn't ready for this shit. I didn't know much about the Fae, but everything I'd learned so far was that they all wanted me dead. They wanted Fergus dead too.

"How do you know they won't kill Fergus or me?"

"Because my father has already started changing the laws. It's now illegal to kill a guardian for loving their charge. He's still working on opening the portal. You can help with that, Serafina. We need you."

I sighed. I needed to put on my big girl panties and do this. Once this was over, I was taking a bubble bath with Skoll and playing with my men.

"Okay, let's do this."

Fergus wrapped his arms around my waist.

"The Fae are friendly people, my Ena."

"If they aren't, I'll just go full demon and gore them with my horn," Amduscias said.

"Yeah, I'll rip their fucking heads off," Roman said.

I held up my hand.

"How about we not kill anyone in the Fae realm just yet?"

My father didn't have me open the portal since I hadn't been to the Fae realm yet, but I'd been practicing opening portals all over the place now that he'd taught me. I was sure I was getting annoying with it. I was portalling from upstairs to downstairs, but it was just so fucking cool I could do that.

We all let Eiltan go in first, and I was shocked when I stepped through. If anyone cared enough about me topside to have thrown me a surprise party, that's basically what I just walked into—a big, fairy surprise party.

I stepped into this vast ballroom that looked like some set in a fantasy movie, and Fae were standing all over the place. The crowd broke, and I could see a huge carpet leading up to a dais. Holy shit, Ior was sitting on a huge silver throne. Eiltan took my hand and led me up the rug. There was a chair up there for all my mates and me too.

I was trying not to turn purple as all these Fae lords and ladies started clapping on my way up. With my luck, I would trip and faceplant right in the middle of this fancy gold carpet and embarrass myself. I wasn't even dressed right for this. All the Fae were dressed in silver and light blue. I was in a black corset and a long purple skirt. My men were all in black too. They looked sexy as fuck, but we all looked like we came straight from Hell.

Ior stood when he saw me and gave me this little bow.

"Princess Serafina Sunshadow!" he yelled, introducing me.

Okay, we hadn't talked about that. We hadn't talked about me taking their last name, and they knew I didn't want to be a princess. I would not make a scene, but we would have to talk later. Ior introduced all my men, then indicated we should sit. He started pacing in front of his throne.

"My granddaughter and her mates are responsible for helping bring a remedy to our people. I think that means it's high time we change how we look at halflings. She's more than proven herself resourceful and brave. She captured Zepar single handedly, and she helped stop a revolution in Hell. That's more than some Fae can say they have done in their lifetime, and she's quite young.

"So, I say to you, why are we keeping the door to the Fae realm closed? Why are we not mixing with other supernaturals? Fate has chosen to mate her with a wolf, a Vampire, a demon, and her guardian loves her too. We Fae don't deny ourselves love when it comes to other Fae. How do we know we can't have the same happiness she has outside of our realm?"

I closed my eyes. I was waiting for screams of judgment. I was waiting for someone to start yelling to kill both me and Fergus. I opened my eye a crack when it didn't happen. No, they started clapping and hooting. These snooty Fae were acting like Americans at a football game at the idea. Well, I'll be totally fucked. Ior addressed the crowd again when they started to die down.

"Serafina doesn't want to take the throne—"

They actually started booing. Did they seriously want me as their queen? Serafina, the street urchin, as the queen of the Fae? I'd give it a week before they were screaming for my head. I was bound to fuck up and kill the wrong person. Besides, I was a psycho, and you never wanted a psychopath running a country. History had taught us that much.

"Now, now," Ior said. "She doesn't want to be queen, but she has agreed to be the ambassador for any halflings born topside. Eiltan will be taking over as king as soon as things are running smoothly, and there's someone he'd like to introduce you to. Eiltan?"

Eiltan held out his hand, and a beautiful Fae woman came out. Seriously, she was so pretty she made every other Fae in the room pale in comparison, and there were a lot of lovely people here.

"I believe you all know Teafa. I've been in love with her for years, and she's agreed to be my wife. We will start working on the next heir to the Fae throne as soon as we are wed. I hope Serafina will guide her little brothers and sisters."

When did he do this? When did he have time to propose, and why didn't he tell me? And little brothers and sisters? Sign me the fuck up. I'd always wanted siblings. It sounded like I would be making a lot more trips to the Fae realm than I thought. I would have a family—with a dad, a stepmom, and brothers and sisters. I couldn't even imagine that. Would she love me like she did her own children?

Teafa turned and gave me a kind smile.

"I hope you'll stick around and give me more time to get to know you."

Oh, my god, was I about to cry? Right in front of all these fairies? I sniffled and tried to control myself. Fergus grabbed one hand, and Amduscias grabbed the other. Get it under control, Serafina. Don't cry in front of the Fae.

"I'd like that," I said once I was sure I would not start ugly crying in front of all these people.

"I have a few more announcements," Ior said. "Serafina has also discovered some unsettling developments with our business venture Scorchwood Supernatural Penitentiary. A coven has been diverting funds and experimenting on patients. They were even framing our elemental offspring hoping to steal magic.

"I'm happy to report we've overturned the charges on all the elementals that were framed. They have all returned to their lives topside. We have a team reviewing the sentence of every prisoner in Scorchwood at the moment. Some prisoners who have been there a long time have been given cruel and unusual punishments with some things that have come to light.

"We have a team reviewing sentences now. The men you see sitting on stage right now have been granted a pardon. They have paid for their crimes, and they are now free to come and go as they please. This is also being done for every inmate in Scorchwood. More dangerous prisoners have been moved to the maximum-security prison Silverhold Detention Center for the Magically Delinquent, and some have been moved to other facilities while we review their sentences.

"The board is still deciding if we will close Scorchwood or use the funds recovered from Warden Skinner to do the necessary upgrades. These upgrades will take years as they should have been done gradually over decades.

"The demons have allowed us to keep the prison there as long as demons staff it if it reopens. There will be a demon warden, and the guards should be a mix of demons and other supernaturals. I agree with this. If there had been more oversight, this never would have happened, and I take full responsibility for that. If we are going to have business ventures in other realms, we need to include the inhabitants and have our people on staff. Now, let us celebrate!"

The crowd went wild, but I needed a minute to process. Were we all free now? My guys were free too. We could go anywhere. There were still parts of Hell I wanted to explore, and my father wanted to show us the Fae realm. There were also plenty of places topside that I wanted to see. This was all open to me now. Amazing.

This music started playing, and I'd never heard music like that before. My preference was Norwegian death metal, but there was something eerie about the violins, cellos, and flutes playing with the drums and electric guitars. I liked it. Could I buy Fae music CDs here? I didn't even know what kind of currency they used in the Fae realm. I knew I didn't have any, but maybe my father would spot me some to buy some music.

Amduscias and Fergus pulled me to my feet.

"Dance with us."

I rarely danced, but I was digging the vibe from this music. I ended up dancing with all of them. Amduscias and Fergus danced like knights out of an old movie. They spun me all over the floor, and Fergus even dipped me. There was something hugely erotic about getting dipped by a massive blond Fae to this music. I would have to attack him later.

Skoll just grabbed my waist and swayed with me. I rested my head on his chest and listened to his heartbeat. This was nice. I could do this again. Roman danced like a total maniac. He reminded me of some college kid strung out on LSD head banging at a rave. The Fae on the dance floor gave him a considerable berth, but I was laughing and having a blast the entire time.

I danced with a few other Fae and my father. All I knew about the Fae were that they were snobs, but this visit proved that wrong. They were all so lovely to me. They were humble and grateful to me for what I had done with Zepar. They weren't huge ass kissers, and I liked that. They were able to thank me in a way that I wasn't totally uncomfortable.

By the time the night wound down, I was exhausted and had had a blast. Eiltan led me to my quarters. Ior must have done this while we were in Hell, and I had no idea when he had the time. They decked my suite out almost like a topside bedroom, and the bed was big enough for all of us.

"I didn't know what kind of music you listened to, but the television gets all Fae and topside channels."

"Actually, I loved the Fae music that played at the celebration. Is there any way I could get copies of some music?"

Eiltan beamed at me.

"I'll get you a flash drive full of the best Fae music. Deal?"

"Deal. How did you have time to propose with everything going on?" I said, smacking his arm.

Eiltan looked embarrassed.

"I met Teafa fifteen years ago. I proposed to her ten years

ago. We made a promise. When I became king, we would wed. I told her about you as soon as I found out you were in Scorchwood. We tried to figure a way to get you out together, but that was when we thought you were guilty."

"I'm happy for you. She looks like she loves you."

"She'll love you too, Serafina. She's a gentle woman with a lot of love in her heart."

"I expect lots of baby brothers and sisters to corrupt."

He grinned at me.

"Watch it, or you'll be babysitting the little hellions."

Was it wrong that I actually wanted to?

SERAFINA

Okay, the Fae realm was absolutely gorgeous. It looked like a cross between a fantasy movie and a vacation brochure to some paradise island. They made the houses out of some stone that shone iridescent silver and blue in the light, and the trees all had purple leaves. Eiltan brought us all over the place, and the people were so lovely to us. Fergus said the Fae could be snobby, but I didn't see that at all.

I got my day alone with Fergus in the Fae realm. Amduscias, Skoll, and Roman spent a day at the beach while Fergus took me on this tour. He took me to this little Fae restaurant where they served the most fantastic food, and then he took me to get some version of Fae gelato. It wasn't ice cream, and it wasn't gelato. I just knew it was cold, creamy goodness, and I wanted every flavor in the shop.

We made love for hours when we got back to the castle,

and it was even more amazing than in my dreams. He was *mine* now. They were all mine.

By the time we left, Ior had passed several laws to open the door to topside, and I'd gotten to know my family better. I liked Teafa, and I thought we would get along just fine. My father was so different than I thought he would be. He was a total hardass when I watched him in meetings about passing laws, but when we were alone, he was funny and a little goofy. He had a nasty sense of humor that spoke to my inner psychopath. The guys liked him too, and Eiltan always made everyone feel included.

I felt a little sad when we left. I'd made a few friends here, and I loved the food and music. Amduscias had visited with the chef at Ior's castle to get recipes to bring back, and Eiltan gave me a flash drive full of music and an e-reader full of books by Fae authors. He also gave me two little devices to plug into the laptop and television that would allow us to access Fae televisions shows in Hell. I'd started watching some series on the Fae version of Netflix, and I was dying to know how it ended.

When we got back to Hell, we reported straight to Bael. I asked about Warden Skinner because I was still pissed about getting shot, even if the water demon healed me quickly, and it didn't hurt anymore.

"I think she's told us everything she knows. We've gone through everything at her apartment and what was left at the castle. Their coven is gone. I'm letting Solron blow off some steam, and then I will kill her slowly."

"Can I blow off some steam too?" I asked.

"No, dear. You had your fun with the rest of the coven. It's Solron's turn to play, but I do have a gift for you, my dear. We all feel bad Zepar's execution was ruined when you went through the trouble of planning something so fitting. Solron likes you and wants to get to know you better. She wants to plan an execution with you because she likes your style. What do you say? Can Solron get her jollies torturing the Warden, then you can both have fun planning her execution? There won't be a sniper there to ruin it this time."

I said I was putting Elemental Batwoman behind me after the coven was dead, but Warden Skinner was their High Priestess, and I didn't think I would ever stop being mad they fucking shot me. Who brought guns to a magic fight, anyway? Evil witches and warlocks who framed people and experimented on them, that's who.

"Is Solron a twisted fuck?" I asked.

Bael gave me this wicked grin.

"She's such a twisted fuck, I'm probably going to make her my queen."

"Excellent. Then I like your idea, and I can see us becoming great friends."

"Good. Maybe you can rein her in a little."

Not likely, but Bael could believe that all he wanted.

"How was the Fae realm? Are treatments going well?"

Fergus snapped to attention. Like I was the new halfling ambassador since Fergus was currently the only full Fae resident in Hell, he was Hell's new ambassador to the Fae realm. I wasn't all that sure about it until we got to the Fae realm and I saw no one would kill him. It warmed my little black heart that all the Fae accepted him, and some of them were kissing his ass because they heard the stories about his heroics when he was alive. Those Fae men and women who were hitting on him needed to step off though.

"Treatments are going well. The Fae physicians synthesized it and turn it into an aerosol. We can administer it as a simple nostril spray. They are working on getting it out to the more rural areas of the Fae realm now. The women who have already received the treatment are already trying to conceive."

"Wonderful. Demons love babies, and what Zepar did was incomprehensible. What about opening the door to the Fae realm?"

"The law passed, but all of that has to be worked out with topside. Times have changed since the last time the door was open. People don't even like immigrants from other countries nowadays. Opening up a door to another realm may cause riots if it's not done correctly. The Fae could be in danger when they come through if we do not introduce them in the right way. It won't be like last time where they were new and interesting. There will be people who are suspicious of their motives for returning this time."

I knew that, and so did Fergus, but it was Eiltan who brought all that to the table. Before I met him and started finding out about him, I thought he was some asshole playboy who kept tripping and ending up with his dick in women while he was framing elementals and experimenting on them.

That ended up totally wrong. While I was in the Fae realm, I spent some time alone with him. He told me all about my mother, and he really loved her. He even showed me pictures of her. Aside from my ears, I looked just like my father, but he was able to tell me little things I got from her.

It seems as if even though I never met her, we had the same taste in food. She liked to soothe her nerves with heavy metal too. He told me we laughed the same, and he wished I would laugh more because he enjoyed the sound from both of us. He kept apologizing for not coming back sooner before she disappeared off the grid.

Eiltan wasn't like the way I thought. When he was topside trying to figure out how to fix his mistake, he wasn't just trying to figure out how to defeat Zepar and falling in love. He was networking and watching, trying to figure the best way to open the door when he became king. He just had no idea Ior had been thinking the same thing.

As soon as Eiltan mention that there may be push back, he whipped out this entire presentation on how to introduce the Fae back to the world, so no one thought they had ill intentions coming back. I was pretty impressed. I even had a *that's my dad* moment I was so proud of him.

Fergus was pretty impressed with him too. Fergus wasn't around Fae court when Eiltan was growing up. All he ever heard were rumors that he was irresponsible and would make a rotten king. Fergus was glad to be proved wrong, too, and not just because he was my dad. Fergus was still a Fae, and he wanted what was best for his people.

Bael was just sitting there, nodding.

"How do the Fae intend to spin the Scorchwood angle before they come back? That will be a huge stain on their reputation if people found out they imprisoned their own kind for not coming home, then everything Warden Skinner's coven did."

"There is full transparency in the Fae realm about what Scorchwood started out for. People are understandably upset, but they also understand that it was under a different king. There's no point in punishing Ior for the sins of his ancestors, and we can't bring those Fae back to life. It was decided to keep Scorchwood's origins among the Fae, but go public with everything that happened afterward.

"The Fae will admit fault for not having better oversight in the prison to make sure all the work was actually being done, and that part is true. While Warden Skinner came highly recommended and was voted to her position by an entire board of various supernaturals, the Fae should have been more involved as majority shareholders, and we should have had demons involved. There's a lot of wrong mythos about demons topside, and the Fae were apparently outvoted about demon involvement. We are all horribly sorry, and we should have overridden them."

I held my breath while I waited for Bael to respond. I knew all the kings of Hell were pretty pissed off Scorchwood turned into a commercial enterprise, and they got left out, but I didn't know if that explanation would be good enough for them. Demons had some weird honor code and found the strangest things offensive, considering they unleashed someone like me and put me in charge of two executions. Bael was just like, hey, you can kill these people in whatever manner you want, and the more fucked up it was, the more they liked it. But they got offended if you used the wrong fork at dinner or did a business deal dishonorably.

Bael just nodded.

"I can understand that. We pass misinformation for a reason, and it was bound to bite us in the ass, eventually."

Amduscias looked like he was dying to speak, but he was waiting for Bael to finish. He finally just blurted it out.

"What about Finn's intel? It still doesn't sit right with me that Saleos died to prove a point. I don't want him to die in vain, especially since his mate was taken from him so horrifically. He is right. What's being done to protect our smoke and flame demons now that Saleos was willing to die for them?"

"It's already in the works, son. Finn had a wonderful idea, and he will make an excellent addition to Hell. Solron is excellent with hacking. She's been locating any sources of

Bitter Woundwort around the world. It's notoriously tricky to grow. Only experienced botanists have been able to manage it, and it's usually done in greenhouses no one knows about. Most witches and warlocks look down on demon summoning too, and they don't want it grown either.

"Finn has offered to assemble a team of sympathetic witches and warlocks to use Solron's intel to wipe all traces of that foul herb off the earth. Charley has offered to help. She might be small, but she's quite a powerful witch. Those two will make quite the power couple in Hell. Finn has already joined their coven, and I gave them a house for helping with the rebellion. Finn is quite the inventor. I heard about the device he used in Romania. I've already given him a job."

I was happy for Charley. I'd still be under Rathmore's spell in Scorchwood if it weren't for her, and so would Roman. I was glad she was out, and I was glad she found someone. I was also glad Finn was proving resourceful. I didn't like the fact that Saleos died either. I understood why he had to, but I hated that it came to that.

I didn't know a damned thing about demon summoning because I didn't do it, but I was learning when witches and warlocks wanted to stir up some shit, they weren't above torturing and killing demons to get what they wanted. I'd met some friendly demons, and I didn't want any of them killed just because some witch got greedy. This was a splendid thing.

Bael clapped his hands.

"Go home, all of you. Enjoy Hell and live your lives. The rebellion is over, we've figured out how to save our smoke and flame demons, the Fae are cured, and no one will have to experience Scorchwood the way you did ever again. Let

Finn and his team handle wiping out any way to summon demons. Let the Fae handle their reemergence into the world. You've done enough. Focus on you for now."

Was this it? Was it finally over, and we could make a home now? It felt like we had been fighting for so long. I was sure going to try to relax and find out.

SERAFINA

Epilogue

Bael was right. It was mostly over. That didn't mean all of us jailbirds didn't spend an entire year looking over our shoulders waiting for some dirty witches or demon royalty to act up again. Eventually, we all just fell into this natural pace where having a beautiful, dull day where we pigged out on food and shagged like bunnies seemed like the norm.

I did say mostly over. All the major players in the plots and subplots were dead. Solron and I had many wonderful girl's nights out at this little demon bar, planning how we would kill Warden Skinner. Solron was now one of my best friends right up there with Charley. Let's just say when Solron and I decided on how Warden Skinner would die, it was *explosive.*

It took a few years for Finn and his team to make it

impossible for anyone to ever summon a demon again, but it happened. There was this massive block party in Hell when it did. Demons knew how to party, and we all got so drunk that night I had regrets about how much I drank for an entire week. But I had so much fun.

Eiltan's plan to reintroduce the Fae worked, but it ended up being a five-year campaign before most people felt okay with the Fae being back. I would have thought the Fae would have dropped it when they realized they would not be celebrated again, and they were getting pushback, but they really wanted this to work, and they just tried harder.

When the Fae started coming through, they worked hard at integrating, and like they promised, elementals were allowed through the door if they wanted to visit and live there. From what my father told me on my visits with him, the elementals were only allowed to stay if they weren't insufferable assholes like they were when I lived topside, and they quickly learned rules actually did apply to them in the Fae realm.

I got to attend a Fae royal wedding when my father married Teafa. It was beautiful and unlike anything I'd ever seen before. The remedy was working quite well because I now had four half-siblings I adored to death. My little brother was the next Fae king, and I was having so much fun corrupting him. I think Teafa wanted to strangle me when he started spouting profanities and set something on fire for fun.

Scorchwood was slowly coming along, but doing all the updates that were needed would take time. Bael appointed the one warden he could trust to keep things in order. Solron would be the new warden of Scorchwood, and I already knew there would be no hanky panky going on there under her watch.

As for me, Elemental Batwoman was truly retired. I was still one twisted mother fucker, but I wasn't killing the bad guys anymore. I found a more kinky outlet in Amduscias's dungeon, and it was so much fun. Amduscias taught me how to be a Domme, and we played so many games with Roman. Roman was a bit of a brat. I think we all knew sometimes he did things just because he knew he would end up getting punished. If I was totally honest, I loved it when Roman misbehaved.

I was closer than ever with Skoll. He might be some colossal Alpha wolf, but he was such a softie. He loved spoiling me, and I got to the point where I let him do it instead of feeling weird about it. I loved just soaking in the bathtub with him while he scrubbed my back and washed my hair.

Even now, I was still getting a kick out of having Fergus real. Sometimes, I just reached out and touched him just to be sure. Waking up snuggled next to him still felt like this enormous treat. I hoped that never wore off. I hoped I always felt this same feeling in my gut when I saw his beautiful face and realized he was real and all mine.

I'd learned so much from Amduscias. He took us on several vacations all over Hell, and we even went places topside. I *did* eventually become a Duchess of Hell. We had this beautiful ceremony where Bael married all of us together, then an enormous party where I was proclaimed as a Duchess. It still made me uncomfortable that I was now a part of Hell royalty, and I probably would always use the wrong fork at dinner at one of the king's houses.

We had started on a family. We didn't plan on who was getting me pregnant first. We just let it happen naturally. I ended up having Amduscias's child first. I honestly didn't know what kind of child I would have with him since he was fire born, but I ended up with a fiery Pegasus that was just so badass. She was this amazing combination of both of us.

It took time, but our house was soon swarming with children. Fergus helped with all the children because I didn't know the first thing about raising a child with a fire element. They all had to help because I didn't know the first thing about wolf, Vampire, and demon children. My son with Fergus ended up more Fae than halfling. He had pointed ears where I didn't.

We fought hard for it, and yes, we killed, but we were now home, and I'd finally found my family... all of them.

AFTERWORD

Thank you for reading the conclusion to Scorchwood Supernatural Penitentiary. I hoped you enjoyed it as it was a lot of fun to write. I left two Easter Eggs in this book. When I write about demons, I try to use actual demons from demon lore. Amduscias exists in demon history. He can make musical instruments play, and he can turn into a unicorn. Zepar is also another character from demon lore with the power to make women barren.

But did you notice the minor character Barbatos? He's also an actual demon, and he will be a player in My Beautiful Monsters

Also, I mentioned some prisoners from Scorchwood are being shipped off to Silverhold Detention Center for the Magically Delinquent. That series will feature a badass Kitsune thief.